THESE YEARS OF PROMISE

A NOVEL

by

NICK HARRISON
With Kenneth Sollitt

Sunrise Books
1707 E Street
Eureka, California 95501

Printed in the United States of America

Library of Congress Catalog Card Number
87-82630

ISBN 0-940652-05-6

Dedicated
To
Kenneth Sollitt
The man who brought us the
Bullard Family

Grateful acknowledgement is made to the North
Coast Writers for their practical advice and assist-
ance, and particularly Alice Sharpe for her help
with the manuscript. I would also like to thank my
wife, Beverly, my daughters, my parents, and Mike
and Judy Phillips for their encouragement and support, as well as Donna Janke for her typing efforts.
Thank you all!

PUBLISHER'S PREFACE

Several years ago we came across a remarkable book, published in 1971, which received little exposure. It told of life on the rough rugged prairie of Iowa in the late 1800's, of the brave Bullard family and their move to the flat vacant land near Stebbinsville, and particularly it was the story of wife and mother Molly Bullard as seen through the eyes of the second Bullard daughter, Ann. The inner strength Molly exhibited in the face of continued hardship was an example of the faith of our pioneering ancestors.

We decided that book, *Remember the Days*, deserved another chance at publication, and so we reissued it in two shorter volumes---*This Rough New Land* and *Our Changing Lives*, as the first two of what we called our Ann of the Prairie series.

So successful were they that we soon envisioned a continuation of the life of the Bullard family---this time with more focus on Ann herself as she enters young womanhood at the turn of the century. Out of that vision comes this third book, *These Years of Promise*.

Kenneth Sollitt, the author of the first two books, did tremendous research on the era, setting, and lifestyle of Iowa in the late nineteenth century. Many of the letters we receive from readers note the ring of authenticity found in Ann of the Prairie. After a strong beginning, however, he was unable to progress beyond the beginning of this third volume because of health reasons. The book was therefore written and the project thus brought to completion by our editor, Nick Harrison, who first discovered the original book and believed in the story of the Bullard family. We are pleased with the result. Mr. Harrison's writing ability and Mr. Sollitt's adaptability were able to blend harmoniously to produce a book which, we feel, retains the flavor and style of real life at the turn of the century.

These Years of Promise opens with Ann facing a new life, preparing to leave her beloved prairie to become a student at the Sioux City Academy for Young Women. Readers have previously known the voice of Ann Bullard as a little girl and as a growing teenager. Now though, she is a young lady at the beginning of a new phase of life. We hope you'll see in her the emergence of the woman who will one day be the aunt to Ken, the young lad in the prologue of *This Rough New Land.*

PROLOGUE

In every man or woman's life there comes a certain unforgettable season when circumstances arrange themselves so as to present decisions which will affect the entire course of one's destiny. How one chooses at that moment later proves to be the spring from which the waters of the future flow.

In the summer of 1896 I was just ready to turn seventeen. I had finished as much education as any Bullard had ever had. I was in love with a wonderful young man, the Reverend (how he disapproved of that formal title!) Martin Pritchard. He had proposed and I had accepted. What remained but to simply marry and raise a family? Certainly it was the tradition among my peers to do so.

But I wanted something else.

I wanted to be a writer someday---and I wanted to learn. So, I had a choice---I could delay our marriage for four years and gain my education. Or I could follow the normal course of events for most young women my age and marry.

I was advised by many people regarding my choice. Some, notably my older married sister Elsie, urged me to forgo the education---why would a woman with a man waiting consider otherwise? Others, such as my very wise mother, my friends James and Julia Evans and, blessedly, my Martin, encouraged me to get as much education as I wanted.

So, with some trepidation, some eagerness, and some very adolescent confusion, I chose the Academy.

I went for an education. But little did I realize that the real education we receive in life can never be learned from books and lectures, no matter how excellent. Instead, through the new experiences and friendships I found in Sioux City, and through the ever present trials of life that were presented to me during those four years, I was to learn a great deal about what being an adult woman, and indeed a human being, was all about.

The excitement of being young is a universal joy. To have been young and expectant of life's treasures as a new century was about to dawn was all the more glamorous---especially for someone who fancied herself a writer. During those four years I purposed to develop those qualities I thought I possessed which would make me a writer. I noticed, I remembered, and I wrote.

Life comes to us but once. Sadly, few people savor the taste of their early adult years, the years of promise. They think to live life fully they must plow doggedly ahead without regard to remembrance. I've found, to the contrary, that the great joys and sorrows of life can be captured---to be appreciated again and again and to be passed on to those who follow as a reminder of the truth of the saying, "I shall not pass this way again."

I went to the Academy a young impressionable woman. And my time there was indeed one of those unforgettable seasons from whence was to flow the rest of my life.

CHAPTER 1
AUGUST 1896

It seemed to be the hottest day of the year when I found myself packing for the train ride to Sioux City the following morning. The sky was clear and it was quiet outside. It was a pleasant change from the harsh dust storm of the day before which had left a film on every window in Stebbinsville.

I looked out my upstairs window and watched Papa for a minute as he dutifully supervised Vina and Lucy in cleanup. Even little Mae was helping by bringing buckets of clean water from the house and emptying the dirty water on Mama's bed of pink roses.

Papa's voice had its usual bossy sting as he lifted one of his crutches and pointed at the window Lucy was working on. "Streaks to the left, young lady; watch for streaks."

I supposed I should have been relieved to have been spared the work and his vexation. I'm sure he would rather have been doing the work himself, but until he was fully mended from his accident at the County Fair his usefulness was limited to supervising others. And, of course, that seemed to make him all the more ornery. But as I listened to his voice, I tried to memorize the sound of it. I supposed I'd even get to missing that in a few days! I knew too I'd dearly miss the smell from Mama's bread setting out to cool that now hung in the air.

I looked around me. All my life I had longed for a

room of my own, and now that I had had one for only three months I was giving it up. Soon I would be sharing a room with some other girl at the Academy.

There seemed to be so many things to miss---how could I bear it? I remembered six years earlier when we left our wonderful home in Saunemin. All of us, save Papa, were sure nothing could equal our happiness there. But it did. Our new friends, our farm, the Literary Society, the church---they had all come to be even greater for us here in Iowa. Elsie had met and married Jed here. Had it not been for the move, I would never have met Martin ---dear Martin. How was I to bear four years waiting to marry? And yet, if leaving Stebbinsville for a while would bring me but half the happiness as had our move from Illinois, it would be more than enough.

I closed my carpet bag and set it on the floor with the rest of the luggage. Mama knocked once, then came in. I looked at her the way I had tried to listen to Papa's voice, trying to capture her face, her hair, her smile. Oh, it was going to be hard to leave!

"Finished so soon?" Mama asked.

"I suppose so. I'm probably forgetting something and I'll remember it as soon as I get on the train," I said smiling.

"Would you be available to help with some pies in the kitchen?"

"Sure, Mama," I answered. I needed something to keep occupied this last day. I wanted it to be a good day---I didn't want to mope around the house.

As Mama and I worked, it was, for the first time I could remember, an easy pace Mama set. Usually we were in a hurry to put food on the table for threshers, or to make sure Papa had his supper on time. But now it was as though the baking was just an excuse for us to be together, to talk, then to be quiet and silently come to understand the separation ahead.

Finally I said, "Mama, I'll be home at Thanksgiving. It's not like I'm going away to be a missionary in Africa. And the train runs twice a day. If you need me I can be home in hours."

"I know dear. But until your own daughter leaves home years from now, you can't know what it feels like to have your children get out on their own. I accepted it when Elsie married Jed because life was hard for us then, and I almost felt relief for her. I was just too busy to let my mind run on it. But with you, it's different. You're not just a few miles away settling in your own home with a husband and a future. I know how much this education means to you, and I certainly want you to have it, but Papa is some right when he talks about a woman's place being in a home with her family."

"Mama, Martin and I will marry and have a family. But being a minister's wife is all the more reason to go to college. I want to be a real helpmeet to him."

Just then Papa and the girls came in boasting about the fine warm weather.

"Just right for a picnic, Molly," Papa said with a wink. Lucy and Mae joined in the chorus, "Oh Mama, could we, could we?" Mama was bent over the oven taking out a hot apple pie, and as she rose with the steaming masterpiece she said, "Why do you think I've been baking pies?"

We spent the afternoon on the banks of Mercy Creek with Vina, Lucy and Mae venturing in and out of the cool waters. The summer Iowa heat was at its driest. I wanted to go in the water too, but felt I should start being a young woman now, not a silly girl who waded in creeks. Instead I sat and talked with Mama and Papa. I hoped my going away would soften Papa some. He seemed to speak more kindly to me now, and sometimes treated me as if he almost cared about me. Mama had always said that men in their hardiness had little time for emotion. They expressed their love in more material ways---providing the necessities for their loved ones. But I was glad that Martin could show me and tell me he cared for me in the ways I needed. I wished that for Mama. Yet I knew she so loved Papa that to her it was enough just to be Mrs. Sam Bullard.

As night fell and we came home hot and tired, we had a surprise waiting for us on the front porch. Mr. and Mrs. Evans sat on the swing rocking gently.

"Well, it's about time," Mr. Evans said. "Keep company waiting often like this and you'll find yourselves very lonely!"

We showed them into the house and Mama served them pie. Then they presented me with a going away gift that would have far more importance in my life than any of us could have guessed that night.

As I unwrapped it I knew by the shape it was a book ---Mr. Evans had never given me a present that hadn't been a book. It was like an unspoken tradition which still carried weight with my heart. The Evanses were my closest friends in the world. She had been my teacher, he had started me on the quest to learn through the loan of books and our weekly discussions that followed. Their presence that night was yet another painful reminder of all I'd be leaving behind.

As I stripped away the last of the wrapping I discovered a large blue fabric book with ornate gold letters stamped on the cover: Journal. The inside cover lining was beautiful patterned paper of fleur de leis. The first blank page was inscribed,

To our Ann,
a very special young woman.
May this journal be the inception
of a long and satisfying life of writing.
All our love,
James and Julia Evans
August 31, 1896

Lucy was standing by my side, and she reached over and ran her fingers across the page as if it was gold. "It's so pretty," she said. "Surely you're not going to mark in it?"

The Evanses laughed. "But she must," Mrs. Evans said. "We're counting on Ann to become a great writer someday."

4

"---And make us all famous," Mr. Evans continued.

Mae scanned the pages and said, "But this isn't a book. It's empty. There's no pictures and no writing."

Mama answered her. "Mae, the 'book' is in Ann, and what her life will be. She will write the words to make a book that maybe someday people will read."

I felt tears starting to fill my eyes, so I reached over and hugged Mr. and Mrs. Evans to thank them.

As they stood to leave, Mrs. Evans said, "One final thing, Ann. You must begin to think of us as James and Julia. You're a college woman now, an adult. It sounds too formal for you to address us as 'Mr. and Mrs.' any longer."

"But I couldn't. How could I ever call one of my teachers by her first name?" I replied.

"I'm not your teacher anymore, dear."

She kissed me on the cheek and as they turned to leave, Mr. Evans---James---turned and smiled at me the same way he had so many Saturday mornings when I had delivered his milk and eggs. For a moment my heart was reminded of how much I had thought I loved him. And as Mama had said, it was a kind of love, a special kind of love, different from the way a married woman loves her husband, but none the less real.

I lay awake in bed a long time that night. I was thinking that even when I came home for vacations, it wouldn't be the same as it was this one last night. I could never again be a little girl snuggled safely in bed, with Mama and Papa downstairs to do all the worrying and caring. From now on I would be almost like a guest. It was that way with Elsie now that she had married Jed. She was still my sister, Mama and Papa's daughter, but now she lived somewhere else. She was Jed Miller's wife, and because of that, she would never quite be the same big sister to me she once had.

Poor Vina! Now she would be the oldest at home. The duties of the eldest would fall to her. How different she was from me. I was serious and quiet and tried so hard to be obedient. Vina was funny and always trying to find something to make her laugh. I was sure she and Papa would be facing many a battle with me away.

Sleep finally came, but I was the first awake in the morning, except for Papa who was already hovered over a cup of steaming coffee at the breakfast table. As I came down the stairs he turned briefly to me and then back to his coffee. I sensed that he felt awkward---the two of us alone on the morning I was to leave. He thought he should say something of a "best wishes" nature, and yet those kinds of words never came easy for Papa. He could joke with us girls, he could boss us, or punish us. But he never could get the hang of talking seriously with us the way Mama could.

It was awkward for me too. But I went over and kissed his forehead.

"Well Papa, in a few hours I'll be gone. Just think of the money you can save on food now!" I said.

Papa picked up the hint and started in. "Food! Why I'll do more'n save on food. No more fool money spent on cloth for new dresses. No waitin' and wonderin' where you and Martin are and what you're up to at all hours. Besides, sending you off to college sure isn't saving us any money that I know. Why that tuition is just plain robbery."

We lapsed into strained silence. Then Papa added, "But I reckon we'll get by. One sure benefit is there'll be one less piece of your Ma's pie to share." He reached across the table to cut a piece to wash down with his coffee.

I wished he hadn't mentioned the money. Mama had assured me there was money from Grandpa's will that would provide for all four years of school. But the fact remained, it was money that Papa could have spent on something more practical than my dream of an education.

Of course Papa wouldn't have said what he did in Mama's presence, she had already reminded him that it was her money to spend, and that Grandpa would have heartily approved of my plans.

6

Still, it made me all the more eager to make the next four years worthwhile.

In a few moments Mama came down and poured herself some coffee and asked again what time my train was to leave, though she knew as well as I.

"At ten past eight, Mama," I answered. I glanced at the chime clock over the mantle---it was a little after six. At once I realized how much I'd miss the clear sound of that clock striking the hour. Would I be able to sleep without the reassuring presence that had filled my nights for so many years?

Mama started fixing breakfast, though I insisted on just a piece of pie. I was too excited to eat one of Mama's filling Iowa breakfasts. Instead, when my pie was gone and while the others ate, I went back upstairs to gather my bags and take a last look at the view from my window. I raised the sash and looked over the living prairie just beyond town. Prairie was home to me. I knew that no matter how long I stayed in the city, I could never consider myself other than a prairie girl at heart.

I loved these late summer days, often so quiet, so still the calm is disturbing. Nothing in nature moves, but you have the feeling that something, perhaps everything, is about to go into motion. The silence seems ready to whisper, maybe even shout. And the stillness of the moment is atingle with suspense and uncertainty. As I took one last look at the motionless painted world beyond, I felt a strange mingling of dread and anticipation within me.

Beneath my window, the tree was still green. It was too early for it to be otherwise. I found myself staring at it, and as I watched, one yellow leaf let go and fluttered to the ground. Nothing visible had separated it from the family of leaves it was deserting. There was no wind. It simply let go, just as I was letting go of things dear and familiar, to be tossed by unknown adventures I had no way of anticipating. Since that day I have thought of that brave leaf many times as a symbol of my own life at that moment.

7

Soon the spell of the realization was broken as Vina called from the foot of the stairs, "Ann, we're almost ready to go."

I put on my hat, with its modest straw braid decorated with bows of white, pink, and maize. I let a little of my chestnut brown hair stick out from under it. I glanced quickly in the mirror and thought to myself, "a dead leaf falling? No! A butterfly emerging from a cocoon into a whole big beautiful world to explore."

Then I walked out of my room, and down the stairs toward my future.

The schedule was for Jed and Elsie to drive in from their farm with Grandma Dauber, who had been spending some days with them. She and Papa seemed almost in rivalry over who could dote on little Davey the most. On their way, they were to pick up Martin, who, along with Grandma Dauber, had determined to accompany me to Sioux City. They would settle me into the Academy and then return on the evening train.

When they arrived, Martin piled my bags into the back of Jed and Elsie's spring wagon. Vina, Lucy, and Mae climbed aboard and crowded into the back. Martin helped me up into Mama and Papa's surrey where the four of us would ride to the station together.

I took a last look at the house. Gloryanna, our large tabby, sat on the porch washing herself with great dignity, unaware of the doings of this funny Bullard family to which she belonged. I felt like I should have given her a final squeeze good-bye but it was too late now. Like wading in Mercy Creek, going back to pet a cat would seem childish.

As we rode through town, I took a lingering glance at the places I knew best. Stebbinsville was growing fast and by the time I graduated I was sure it would be a different town. Even now, the frame was up for a lavish new courthouse. I waved to Maggie Bruckner as we passed her on the street, thinking that by the time I saw her again, her baby would be born.

Mama was always one to be early. So it was this first

morning of September all eleven of us stood waiting, Martin holding my hand, Papa glancing up and down the tracks every few minutes like a hungry fisherman checking his hook. Vina, Lucy and Mae were playing "chase" down on the dirt clearing by the station platform. The rest stood quietly making occasional light talk about the good weather for traveling, trains being late, and such. The time for serious talk was past—everyone had given advice and instructions for the past several days. Now we all just waited.

As Grandma predicted, the train was late. Finally we heard the whistle blow from three crossings down. My anticipation and dulling dread increased. At last the train came into view. The rumble and roar of its approach grew louder and soon it screeched to a halt beside us, expressing its weariness with an ear-splitting howl accompanied by the hiss of sweaty steam.

Elsie was the first to give me her final good-bye. My poor sister thought me unreasonable for wanting to go to school, especially, she said, "seeings how you got a man firmly interested in matrimony." As we hugged I saw her fear for me in her eyes and felt it in her embrace.

Jed pecked me on the cheek, little Davey grabbed my neck and held tight. Then, in turn, each of my sisters gave me hearty kisses, with Mae giving me a dandelion she had just picked to help cheer up my new room.

Mama, with tears in her eyes, hugged me next. She said little, but her firm grasp and then gentle release said more than words. Papa was last. His businesslike kiss was quick, but his words, "You get good grades now, y' hear? Make us proud," made me want to do just that. Then he turned to Martin who was starting up the train steps with my bags and said, "Now you see she gets where she aims to go, and no shenanigans. Remember, Martin, she's mine till she's yours."

I thought to myself, "That's one of the nicest things he could have said." I wasn't sure he'd ever claimed me as his own before.

9

Martin deposited my bags aboard the train. He then returned to help Grandma first, then me, up the steps and followed us as we found our seats. I don't know if those on the platform could see us very well through the dirty window. But as I saw them all I tried to memorize the scene of my family bidding me goodbye. I will never forget that picture. It remains as one of the fondest memories in the mental gallery of my family which I treasure to this day.

In spite of the increasing noise of the train engine, now ready to pull away, we waved eagerly and shouted our good-byes, hardly aware of the other passengers aboard the train. I remember vividly the look in Papa's eyes as he waved back.

Then the bell rang, the train grunted and groaned, panted and puffed, and reluctantly left for Sioux City.

CHAPTER 2
SEPTEMBER 1896

The train ride was enjoyable, but for the first few miles the three of us sat in near silence. I suppose it was understandable. Martin had always had his doubts about my going to the Academy, though he supported me in my decision. I was saddened at the thought of being away from him. So there seemed little to be said. The die of this portion of our future had been cast, and it was only left for us to live it out.

After a while Grandma Dauber dozed off. Martin and I still sat side by side, gazing out at the peaceful Iowa landscape rolling by. We seemed able to talk of nothing but trivialities. At length, after a period of quiet, he reached over and took my hand in his.

"I want you to have a good time, Ann," he said. "And I want you to know I'll be thinking of you every day, and praying for you whenever you come into my mind."

I smiled. How I needed to hear that! His words gave me reassurance that everything was going to turn out okay between us.

"But I'll miss you," he went on. "Four years is a long time."

"I'll miss you too," I said. "But I'll see you often...and we'll write."

Now it was his turn to smile. He nodded in agreement, and from then on the somber silence which had seemed to envelop us at first eased, and we spoke more freely.

When a small lunch was served about noon, I was so hungry from skipping breakfast that I devoured it.

At Orange City a young man boarded the train who looked as though he too was leaving home for the first time. He was younger than I, very thin with a protruding Adam's apple and carried a plaid carpetbag. He looked very much like I imagined the character Ichabod Crane. He took a seat near the front of the car, so I was able to watch him from time to time. I wondered if he was going off to the young men's college I had heard about near the outskirts of Sioux City.

It was early afternoon when the train trudged to a halt in front of the Burlington Station in Sioux City. As we stepped off the train I noticed the thin young man getting off at the next door down. He looked curiously both ways as if searching for someone. Then, not finding them, he walked toward Main Street. If he was coming to stay for awhile, he certainly hadn't brought much luggage.

Martin sought out one of the several two-horse cabs waiting at the station platform. Our cabbie knew the Academy and headed us immediately in that direction. As we drove along the streets, there were so many people, so many faces, and not one I knew! The shops were all so big. As we turned one corner, I saw the newspaper office---the Sioux City Journal. If I had the courage, and had been a man, I would have stopped the cab and run in to apply for a job in my after school hours. Perhaps someday, I thought, women will work on newspapers.

And then out of my window I *did* see a familiar face--- it was the skinny young man again. This time he was walking quickly along the street, every once in a while slowing down, looking at the shops as if trying to find a certain one. How curious that I should even consider him a familiar face. I didn't know anything about him, but sometimes I had feelings about people, and wanted to know about them and what their lives were like. I didn't understand it, but Mama told me it was the very

12

thing that would make me a writer some day. Although I never saw the young man again, he was to be the inspiration for the first story I wrote. I imagined his name to be Jimmy Dodge, that he was recently orphaned, and that he had come to Sioux City penniless and looking for a future. In my story, he died after only a year in the city. I have hoped since then, that the young man walking along the street made out better in real life Sioux City than in my imagination.

Our cabbie understood that we were new to town and took the time to point out places of interest. The Federal Building was just under construction. It was a beautiful Florentine architecture, and promised to be a sight for many years. The town clock, Old Ben, would later be installed in its tower.

The magnificent Corn Palace was a monument for farm men such as Papa. It was made of sheaves of grain and red, yellow, and white corn in diverse patterns on a skeleton frame of wood. I knew Martin would wonder at the dome, which was a picture of Mondamin, the Indian god of corn. He was showering Iowa's produce from a horn of plenty. All Martin said was, "We know that every good and perfect gift, including Iowa corn, is from the Father above."

When the cab turned next we found ourselves on Pearl Street, so named, the cabbie told us, for a "colored" woman who had been a cook on one of the boats that docked at the foot of the street where the mighty Missouri River ran. The cabbie pointed to the railroad tracks in the street and said I might want to learn the schedule. The rail through town was a lot cheaper than his cab, he said with a laugh.

It was a wonderful town. I knew I would grow to love it---perhaps not as much as Stebbinsville, but it would be home to me for four years.

Shortly we drew up in front of the Academy, a beautiful three story brick building, my new home. As Martin helped Grandma and me down from the cab, a short man with deep black skin appeared out of nowhere. He helped Martin and the cabbie carry my bags into the large entryway where we were met by a tall, good-looking young woman. Her face was serious as she extended her hand in a businesslike manner and said, "Welcome to Sioux City Academy for Young Women. My name is Rowena Gainesborough. And you would be...?"

I cleared my throat awkwardly and said, "I'm Ann... Ann Bullard. I'm from Stebbinsville."

"Oh, yes," she said with a stiff smile. All my recently acquired womanly confidence wavered in the presence of her polish. "Miss Button has been expecting you. I'll notify her. Please wait here."

Much to my relief the young woman disappeared. Martin paid the cabbie and gave a coin to the black man who left as quickly as he appeared. My eyes followed him, attracted by his beautiful ebony skin. I had rarely seen a black person and had never spoken to one.

Within a minute a large buxom woman with gray hair appeared from an office off the side of the entryway. She seemed more congenial than Rowena Gainesborough. "Miss Bullard, we're so glad you've arrived," she said. "Your room is waiting."

She turned to Martin and Grandma Dauber and I said, "May I present my Grandmother, Emily Dauber, and my fiance, the Reverend Martin Pritchard." Martin cringed as I called him Reverend. He felt it so high-minded for such a simple man as himself. I cringed at calling him my fiance. I'd never used that funny French word before. I wondered if Miss Button could sense how out of place I felt.

"I'm pleased to meet both of you," she said. "Reverend Pritchard, would you mind waiting in the parlor over there," she said with a sweeping gesture to her left. "Visiting gentlemen aren't allowed on the upper floors." With his hat in his hand, Martin sheepishly went into the large parlor and sat uncomfortably in an ornate Windsor chair. In the meantime Miss Button continued speaking to us. "The second floor houses our classrooms---six of them. On the third floor are the dormitory rooms. I have you in room K with a young woman from eastern Iowa, a Bohemian girl, Andela Wersba."

Miss Button led us up wide oak stairs. Her weight seem to work against her progress. "I've been climbing these stairs for years," she said with an infectious laugh. "They get steeper each fall!" Already my fears were subsiding; I was sure I would get along with this delightful woman.

"We have several 'customs' " she said, "---I prefer that word to rules---but whatever you call them, they are observed rather strenuously. We put our lamps out by nine-thirty. Breakfast is promptly at six, lunch at twelve and dinner at six again. Each girl is responsible for keeping her room clean and her bed made. And please ask the folks at home not to send food. There is to be no food kept or eaten in your room---cockroaches can be a problem, you see. We also ask our young ladies to become involved in any one of the several churches in town." She stopped for a second and then added, "but of course your young man is a preacher---that should be an easy 'custom' for you."

Before I could speak Grandma said, "I'm sure you'll find my granddaughter will observe all the customs. She's quite a good girl."

Miss Button smiled. "Of course she is. I say these things to all the young ladies, just so we understand each other right from the start. Believe me, the stories I could tell you about some of the young ladies who've walked these 'hallowed' halls." She rolled her eyes toward the ceiling with a groan. "And I do have Dr. Sinclair, the chairman of the advisory board, to consider. He insists on the utmost propriety from our young women.

"Now, this," she went on, "is the main classroom on the second floor." She opened the door to a large room with beautiful oak walls. Seventy or eighty desks stood in neat rows across the wooden floor. "Once a week, sometimes more, we have assemblies of the whole school."

After brief visits to some of the other classrooms we climbed to the third floor where Miss Button took us straight to my new room.

It was cold and dark, forbidding at first. But Miss Button drew the curtains and lit the lamp, both of which gave the room an immediate warm glow.

The room had two single beds, two commodes, two dressers and two study tables.

The single closet was certainly enough for two girls when one of them had as few clothes as I did.

After a few moments Miss Button said, "Well, I suppose we'd best go back downstairs lest that man of yours think we've dropped off the face of the earth." She again gave her contagious laugh.

When we arrived back at the entryway, Miss Button called out the front door to the black fellow who had helped us unload. "Artemis, please take Miss Bullard's luggage to Room K." Miss Button turned to us and said, "Artemis is the only man allowed on the third floor. When he reaches the landing he gives a signal that he's coming through."

When Artemis reached the third floor I realized that no one could fail to hear the signal. In a high-pitched voice we could hear echoing down the stairwell, "Ooh wee, ooh wee!"

Martin had rejoined us and Grandma and Miss Button discreetly stepped aside to chat while Martin and I had our goodbye.

"If you *ever* need me, I'll come," he said as he kissed my forehead tenderly. I in turn reached up and kissed his lips gently and quickly, and said, "I do love you."

Martin raised his voice to include Grandma, "Well, Mrs. Dauber, I suppose we have a train to catch home. Shall we leave our girl to be educated and return to the outlands from whence we came?"

Grandma pressed my hands in hers, kissed me on the cheek, and gave a final exhortation to write often. They

16

boarded a horse car, and as it took the two of them towards the railway station, I felt alone, really alone, for the first time in my life.

Once they had passed out of my sight, I stood a minute more, then turned away from the street and returned to the lobby, where I stood a moment undecided. Miss Button came to my rescue. She offered to show me her office and then at six to take me to dinner in the dining hall, also on the first floor.

During the evening meal Miss Button introduced me to several of the other students. Like me, most of them were from out of town, some from as far as New York and Massachusetts. Those who came such long distances usually did so because a relative or close acquaintance had preceded them here.

Classes were to start the following Monday. All week young women would be drifting in. I was quite anxious to meet my new roommate. And of course the teachers. So many questions filled my mind. Would I seem a country bumpkin? Were my clothes in fashion? Where would I go to church? And did the school have a library to rival Mr. Evans'?

The young woman who had first greeted me, Rowena Gainesborough, was a returning student from Des Moines. Sioux City was a smaller town than she was used to. She was a lovely young woman, with long yellow hair and deep blue eyes like Elsie's.

She was studying a course at the Academy to prepare her for a law degree at the University. I had never heard of a woman lawyer, nor had it occurred to me any woman might be interested in law. But Rowena was a very clear-minded person and I soon had no doubts she could be quite persuasive before a jury.

Miss Button introduced me to each girl and told them something about me. I was surprised she could remember as much as she did from my application. I know she had a great many to go through, yet she seemed to know as much about me as if mine were the only one she had read. But I came to realize that simply to be another of the wonderful qualities that made her such an excellent matron---she prided herself in being like a mother hen to each of the young women in the Academy.

And in the same way as matronly women like Miss Button are found overseeing Academies, so each school must have a clown of sorts. Ours, I discovered that evening, was Lottie Townsend, from a farm out of Mason City. She was plumpish and hardy and, as time would tell, enjoyed getting a laugh more than getting a good grade. I immediately admired her bright orange hair and blue eyes.

As we sat at the table she turned and whispered to me, "My sister went to this academy a few years ago and came home by Christmas with a husband! I'm going to do the same."

For a minute I said nothing. Was she serious? As she saw my surprise, she said, "Oh, I'll study too. But I really just aim to be a wife and mother, don't you?"

"Well, I...I'm not sure," I said, not daring to tell a practical stranger that I wanted to be a writer more than almost anything.

"Where did your sister meet her husband?" I asked. "At one of the schools in town?"

"At Pilgrim Presbyterian. It's the church in town with the most eligible bachelors," she said with satisfaction.

"I'm engaged," I said, turning back to my dinner, "I guess I'll be here for the education."

Later I found out that Lottie's mother had recently died and her sister and brother-in-law had moved to North Dakota. Her father sold the farm and moved into Mason City where he was courting a prospective new wife. Perhaps, I thought to myself, Lottie wants a husband so she'll have a home to go to. I felt a little sorry for her. I was glad she liked to laugh. Maybe it made the loneliness a little easier.

After dinner, Lottie showed me the "pressing" room in the basement. She also showed me how to use the heavy charcoal iron, a new invention that would replace the irons kept hot on a kitchen range. Imagine an iron with the heat coming from inside of it! The existence of such a contraption amazed me. I could just see my mother's face!

Miss Button then suggested I go to my room to unpack and get some rest. The next day she would assign one of the returning students to show me something of Sioux City. With an arched eyebrow she added, "And show you the places where you're *not* to be seen."

I unpacked slowly, not wanting to be finished too soon. I was too excited to sleep. But soon everything was put away in good order. I sat on my bed. The loneliness I'd felt earlier returned with the stillness. Then I remembered the journal James and Julia Evans had given me. I took it out and wrote these things down to preserve them. Writing about my feelings helped me realize that whatever was making me feel bad would pass. Lottie might laugh to make the loneliness easier. I wrote in my journal.

I undressed and got into my bed with my Bible and turned to Psalms 27 where I read words that helped.

The Lord is my light and my salvation; whom shall I fear?
The Lord is the strength of my life; of whom shall I be afraid?

God was all the light I would be needing, so I blew out the lamp and went to bed.

It was a good bed, but not like my bed at home.

CHAPTER 3
FALL 1896

During the next few days I settled into my new surroundings. Miss Button assigned Rowena Gainesborough the task of taking some of the new students on a day's trip through Sioux City. The places of alarm to Miss Button were taverns on a side of town I was unlikely to visit for any reason. Down by the docks the men who worked the steamboats were often unsavory. Rowena told us of a stabbing that had occurred last winter.

Though she was pleasant enough in her own way, I soon sensed that Rowena and I had less in common than I had hoped. Her legal-oriented mind was much more objective than mine. When she heard I was engaged to a minister and wanted to be a writer I could see disappointment in her face. Rowena, as a third-year student, also made it plain that first-year students were considerably less desirable as friends.

On Friday my roommate arrived. As different as Rowena and I turned out to be, Andela (pronounced to rhyme with Angela) Wersba was as similar to me as I could have wished. Her heritage was different, and she was, if it was possible, quieter than I. But her temperament matched mine almost perfectly. My goal was to express something about life in writing; her's was the gift of art. Although her clothes were even less in number than mine, she had brought easels and paints which more than took up her share of the room. She seemed concerned at first, but I assured her I was glad to be sharing a room with an artist---then I added that perhaps someday she would help me illustrate a story. She smiled deeply but said nothing.

That first night, we sat on our beds talking; reluctantly at first. But as we realized our common shyness, we gradually loosened up and we spoke more freely.

She told me her Bohemian mother and nomadic father had met and married in a small town near Prague. Her father then saved for many years to bring his family to America. Finally the day came when, with several fellow Bohemians, he and his young wife and two toddling daughters came to the new world of promise, America. One of the daughters had died on the ship and was buried at sea. After arriving in New York they simply followed their fellow countrymen west to Iowa, eventually settling in Spillville, a small settlement mostly of immigrants. The town, in fact, had a decidedly European flavor.

On the long trip west the other daughter, the eldest, died and was buried along the trail. Andela was born in Spillville on the farm her father began. Unlike my own Papa, Hansel Wersba settled permanently on the first piece of land he was able to claim. Like our farm, the Wersba soil was rich, and the family, through much hard work, had been able to survive. Andela was quick to praise the rest of the Spillville community--almost all Bohemians.

"We are Americans now---but our language, our culture which seems rooted in our very bones, gives us an unbreakable bond," she said.

She knew, as I did, the work of setting a table for threshers, of working the harvest herself, of tending livestock and then losing all your gain through a sudden change of weather. Yet, like me, I could tell she loved it all in spite of hardship. And as she showed me her paintings of the Iowa landscape I was amazed. Some artists render accurate likenesses in detail but one senses there is still something lacking. Andela's paint-

21

ings carried an extra virtue. They seemed to cause a sense of life to rise up in the breast of the beholder, as if some unseen force had breathed the breath of life into the very canvas.

Though her father appreciated her talent, he scraped enough money together to send her to the Academy rather than to an art school where her talent might be further developed. Andela explained that in the old country physical labor was a virtue. Artistry, though highly regarded, was secondary. Hansel believed that Andela must be educated along business lines and learn to make her way in the world by practical education. If there was time left for painting, fine---but first came a paying job.

Andela was pretty in a simple way. Her quiet but deeply-felt personality was embodied in a willowy frame, her dark eyes and long flowing hair reminded me of the warmth of a day by the river with its enchanting deep pools. Something about Andela made one want to know more about her, yet her attractive shyness covered her like a bridal veil.

I could tell she was here in obedience to her parents' wishes, and that she would do well---but her heart was toward her canvas. Her move to Sioux City was not only her first time away from her home and family but also from their common heritage.

At home there remained a brother, Pavel, fifteen. Though he helped with the farm work as he knew he must, Andela told me his first love was music. What Andela's art meant to her, Pavel's violin was to him.

Andela spoke of Pavel with such sincerity that, as she spoke, I felt I knew him intimately. She could paint not only with oils, but also with words. I wondered if it was a special Bohemian virtue, this family closeness that caused her to talk of Pavel as though he were a saint. It exceeded even the tenderness I felt towards my sisters.

"I worry for Pavel," Andela said. "His music is a treasure---both to the listener and to Pavel himself. I want him to make full use of his talent. I urged my father to save the money used to send me here, save it for the day Pavel could study full time.

"There is a school in Chicago," she said, "the American Conservatory of Music. I wish Pavel to go there. But it is as with me---work first, artistry second---Papa and mother would have him inherit the farm. It's our way that the son takes the mantle from the father in his work. And father has become a fine proud man. From Pavel he expects the same. Besides, the conservatory is very expensive. But I never stop praying for Pavel that he will excel at the violin, and that he will someday go to the school in Chicago."

From several canvases leaning against the wall, Andela picked out a large one and held it up. "This," she said in a soft voice, "is my Pavel."

As with her landscapes, the portrait conveyed more than just the likeness of the young man. There was a quality of life about it which made me feel as if I could immediately set pen to paper and tell his story. Andela's love for her brother was clear just from looking at the painting. It was as if the act of painting gave Andela a way to express her love. When she painted the Iowa countryside it was a way of affixing her love to it. So with her brother.

I understood. Sometimes I felt that by writing, I was able to say things too deep in my heart to be expressed in any other way.

I was surprised that while Andela's features were dark and rather haunting, Pavel's were light, his hair blond and his face angular. He had the look of a gentle young man about him. Yet for their physical differences, Pavel possessed the same quiet shyness about him that Andela did. They both reminded me of the face of a young colt just getting to its feet.

I told Andela about my family. I told her of my Mama and what a wonderful woman she was and about each of my sisters, of Stebbinsville, of Papa and how he sometimes got a "burr under his saddle" that made it hard for us girls to love him as we should. I told her of Martin

23

and my love for him and how I wanted an education partly to better help him in serving a congregation.

Andela was silent a moment and then said, "It will be well for you to succeed as a writer, and for me as an artist, even for Pavel as a musician. But the greatest artist of all is the one who has the gift of serving his fellow man."

We heard slow footsteps down the hall and the voice of Miss Button. "Lights out, young ladies. Lights out." The time had slipped away. It was nine-thirty and those words, accompanied by those measured steps each night, would eventually become as comforting a ritual as listening for Mama's chime clock.

CHAPTER 4
FALL 1896

Monday was registration day.

The morning began with an assembly in the large second floor classroom. Miss Button led in the pledge of allegiance, went over the "customs" of the school again, and finally introduced Dr. Fortney Sinclair to the assembled students.

Dr. Sinclair, as chairman of the board, was the man at whose desk every serious matter was finally settled. As he stood to address us, I noted how tall and thin he appeared, his balding head almost almond shaped. Thin wire rimmed glasses settled far down on his nose. Clearly his presence was warning enough for all of us to stay on our best behavior. I vowed I'd never allow myself the kind of mischief which would warrant a summons for him to call at the Academy.

Dr. Sinclair was a lawyer with an office on Douglas Street. I never understood why he was called "Dr.," yet I had to admit his austere manner confirmed such a title.

I heard little of his speech that morning, preferring to observe all these matters about him. Mostly I heard snatches of admonitions to perfect behavior, good grades, and firm discipline.

After his words Miss Button divided the students into four sections according to their last name initials. A counselor who was assigned each section would interview all the young women and help each plot courses of study. Mine was the section assigned to Mr. Tate, a pudgy little man nearly seventy, a retired merchant. Now serving on the board of directors for the Academy, each fall he offered to help Miss Button with registration duties. Apparently by the force of gravity all the hair nature had given him had fallen and collected on his chin, where it hung precariously in a weather-beaten gray goatee. On the way down, some hair had caught on his ears where it stuck straight out like whiskers on a cat. Yet deep set in his pear-shaped face, a pair of kind brown eyes peered out, which could not help but inspire confidence. He went about his business of counseling me with sympathy and encouragement.

"Where are you from, Miss Bullard?" he asked.

"Stebbinsville," I replied. And while I doubt if he knew where Stebbinsville was, his instincts seemed to tell him that I was a country girl with perhaps dubious aspirations.

"And what do you hope to be when you finish here?" he asked leaning forward.

"I want to be a writer," I said. "A story writer like Louisa May Alcott."

The old man thought for a moment then said, "The field for writers is certainly wide open. There really aren't many good woman writers, and Miss Alcott is proof that a woman can write as well as a man."

I nodded, not knowing what else to say.

He settled back in his chair and acted as if he had news he was reluctant to tell me. "I'm sorry the Academy doesn't offer specific writing courses to help. You see, Miss Bullard," he continued, "since so few women, their place in society being what it is, have the willingness to put forth the effort, or possess the self-discipline learning to write demands, we haven't experienced much need for courses in creative writing."

I felt deserted on an island, my ship of hope having left me. I thought Academies taught everything!

He sensed my frustration. "What other plans have you made for your future?" he asked. I took that to mean writing may not be my future.

I looked down at my hands clasped together in my lap and said, "I'm engaged to be married to a minister. I won't *have* to write for a living."

He paused for a moment then said, "But you *will* have to for your own self-respect and satisfaction?" He did know how I felt after all! "Don't give up on your dream, my dear. Now let me recommend the most helpful courses. You will want to take Mrs. Whitely's course in English Composition," he said as he began filling out the enrollment card.

Mrs. Whitely was a sprite elderly widow who had been teaching writing at the Academy since her husband died a decade earlier. She was a curious woman--- very precise in her manners and, as I was to find out, exacting in the classroom. In her appearance, however, she was always on the edge of disorganization. Her thin hair showed only rudimentary hints of having seen a comb in the morning. Her clothes were usually unkempt. Her favorite pose, which we were to see several times daily, found her resting the fingertips of her right hand on her chin, usually as she thought, sometimes as she spoke, and most frequently as she sat at her desk reading student papers. At such times her skinny fingers danced across her chin in agitation, often in proportion to the quality of the work being read. We could judge an excellent paper by the stillness of her fingers. If the paper was unsatisfactory, the excitement of her fingers increased.

It was during that first week of class when given our beginning writing assignments that I wrote the story of "Jimmy Dodge," the young man I had seen on the train. It was my first try at such a thing and I handed it in with great anxiety. Justified anxiety as it turned out. Mrs. Whitely wrote three pages of sharp correction with the one promising phrase at the end, "though there is much to be corrected in this---I see the seed of possibility here." And I was instructed to rewrite Jimmy Dodge. And rewrite it I did---three times, until finally her short note of only three-fourths of a page read, "It's time to put this aside now. As an exercise, it's done all for you it can. Please see me after class."

Later, with dread and curiosity, I approached her desk. I felt like a child caught in mischief.

Mrs. Whitely started to speak without looking up from the papers she was correcting on her desk. "You want to be a writer, yes?"

"Very much," I answered.

She looked at me and her manner softened. "It's a curious thing to wish to write. In my earlier years, I fancied being an authoress. But...the years pass quickly, all the more so the older you get. And, alas, I remain unpublished. But not for lack of trying." She seemed genuinely touched. She spoke as if I was someone with whom she could share a very precious secret. There was no bitterness in her confession, but she made me feel sorry she hadn't been successful.

"What kinds of stories did you write?" I ventured.

She looked at me and smiled. "I thought I might be something of a writer after Hawthorne's manner. But how foolish I was! Writers must not try to imitate others. They must write what's in *their* hearts. That, young Miss Bullard, is exactly what I wanted to tell you. Write what you know best. It's the best advice any writer can receive."

"Thank you," I said rather uncertainly. Then I added, to make conversation, "I've apparently gotten off to a bad start. I understand the Academy isn't geared to producing authors."

"Good authors, Miss Bullard, produce themselves," she replied with hesitation. "Writers learn to write by writing. Write! Then rewrite. Then rewrite again. And then keep on writing. It's the only way."

Mrs. Whitely's insistence that I "write what I know" sank deep. I wrote it in my journal that night in bold red letters. It was she who convinced me to look to my own experience in Stebbinsville as "grist for the mill," another of her favorite expressions.

It was because of her that I learned to savor every letter from home even more deeply than perhaps I would have otherwise. I loved hearing from Mama, as I did at least twice weekly. Martin, of course, wrote often; his letters added a dimension of spirit only he could give. As mail from home came, from Martin and Mama and from others in Stebbinsville, I was able to appreciate the richness of my being---a heritage that had been unfolding all my life, without my even realizing it. I began to see how God writes our lives just as authors write books. At that young age how I hoped my book, my life, would be a happy one, not a tragedy. Yet something told me that tragedy, when it came to me, could enhance my book-life if I would accept it as from God and not resent it.

Mr. Tate had also enrolled me in the study of "Deportment for Young Ladies," in which Andela and I were classmates. Our instructor was Miss Button who handed us each a manual of etiquette for the "modern young lady," written in her own hand. Andela and I would behave like royalty in class, but when we got to our rooms we would often roll on our beds with laughter. We were, after all, still farm girls and furthermore, though we wanted to have good manners, we liked being farm girls.

After lunch my next class was a beginning business class which, though I never told Papa, for he had insisted I take it, I found rather boring. It was taught by Mr. Rothchilde. Perhaps he was an excellent businessman, but his lectures were boring and prone to induce sleep, especially after a hearty lunch.

I then had a required class in American History which I found interesting, no doubt due to the intriguing way Miss Adams taught. She loved History and made the battles of the Revolution and Civil War come to life.

My final class of the day was English Literature--a class which was like a dessert after a nice meal. The books we read, the papers we wrote, the lectures and discussions, all brought back my Saturday morning rituals from home. With fondness I remembered riding out to Mr. Evans' house to get books which he would select and prepare me for by giving some background on the author and the times in which the book was written. Then he would tell me what kind of things to watch for as I read.

By doing so I had been unconsciously prepared for this class being taught by Mr. Alexander Hoffman. His love for literature paralleled that of Mr. Evans. The influence of those books read and discussed as the afternoon wound down would long have an impact on me.

After classes were over we had nearly two hours to adjourn to our rooms, to read, rest, write letters, and ready ourselves for dinner. The eight instructors at the Academy would head home: Mr. Hoffman to his new wife, Miss Adams to the small cottage where she lived with her aged mother, Mrs. Whitely, to her small house on Piercy Street, and Mr. Rothchilde to the hotel where he kept a suite. Miss Button was the only staff member who lived at the Academy, other than Artemis, and of course Milly, the small black cook.

Supper was one of the best times of the day. The dining hall had twenty round tables where five or six of us could sit together. Usually Andela and I were joined by Lottie Townsend, Marian Sharp, and various other girls. We were expected to finish supper by seven o'clock which usually gave us plenty of time to visit around our tables. From seven to nine was strictly study time. And at nine-thirty we were all to be in our beds with lights out.

As we settled in for the new school year one new student immediately attracted the attention of everyone. Her name was Catherine Bonacre. She was tall, large boned and full bodied, with dark blonde hair and an overwhelming physical presence. Though a first year student, Catherine was twenty years old, nearly the same age as many who would graduate the following June. She had been raised in a banking family in Minneapolis. The previous January, both her parents had died in a fire. She had been sent to live with an uncle in Sioux City, who apparently had little need for her. He suggested, rather forcefully, that an education might be in order, and promptly used a portion of her inheritance to secure her first year's tuition. Though a few girls whose families lived in Sioux City lived at home, several roomed at the Academy. Catherine's uncle made it plain that she too would be best living away from him. It didn't take us long to discover why. Her demeanor was rough and coarse. That she hadn't a male suitor surprised none of us---she took no thought of her appearance and little of her actions. I wondered at once how she could ever study effectively. Yet we were soon to discover that she was a very bright young woman who possessed a natural knowledge which seemed to compensate for the abilities she lacked.

Within weeks, however, there were not a few who had begun to devise ways to avoid her. It was a ruined meal when she sat at our table. No matter how nice we tried to be to her, she continually found ways to belittle us and reject our attempts at friendship. If we tried to study in the parlor while she was there, we found it impossible for her constant complaining. Miss Button spoke to her on three or four occasions, but little changed. Catherine *did*, to her credit, observe the customs, as Miss Button called them, rather well. We soon discovered Catherine's uncle to be a close friend of Dr. Sinclair's, a relationship which seemed to cover a multitude of sins.

It was, of course, Andela who was most patient with her, ascribing legitimate reasons for her behavior. Still, excluding Andela, there was not one girl who could be said to be a friend to Catherine Bonacre.

Those first weeks at the Academy brought mail for me almost every day. Mama always tucked in notes from Vina, Lucy, Mae, and Grandma. And she would add, "Pa sends his best," but there never was a note in his own hand.

Martin was my main link to what was happening out on the farms. With Mama and Papa in town now, they seemed to lose touch with some of our old friends. Others though, like Ethan and Hilda would stop and see Mama and Papa every week when they came to town. Jed and Elsie came to town less frequently, but also stopped in on every visit. The letters became as important reading to me as the most precious of Coleridge's poems, which I was now discovering in Professor Hoffman's class.

I tried to write at least one short letter every night. There were so many I knew wanted to hear from me—the Stones, the Millers, the Evanses, the Bruckners, the Gruders, and of course each of my own family members would expect a word especially for them. Lucy was highly indignant when one of my letters made no inquiry as to her well-being.

The news from home that Fall was scarce. The major event seemed to be that Elsie was to have another baby in the spring. The community was growing. More folks were moving in. And all the young married women were expecting.

Grandma Dauber was settling in Stebbinsville, having sold her home in Roanoke rather quickly. She had chosen to buy a small cottage off Main Street. Papa had offered her a room in our house but she had always been one to want her own privacy. She maintained that families with children still growing needed "visits" from grandparents but only for a short spell.

As for Martin, he was firmly attached to his congregation and they to him. He taught of God's love in such a way as to endear the most hardened sinner to repentance.

CHAPTER 5

Miss Button was vigilant in her insistence that every young woman find and become part of a church. Several of the girls objected, particularly Rowena Gainesborough. Some felt the need for extra study or quiet on Sunday. Others, like Rowena, were fascinated by the current wave of "free thinkers" who decried the doctrines I had come to know and love. Some of the complainers found a home at the Unitarian Unity Church on Tenth St. Eyebrows were further raised when it was made known that the pastor was the Reverend Mary A. Safford, a woman!

Other young women were finding homes in the up and coming church called the Salvation Army. Some stayed with the traditions of their families such as Lydia Lindblom and Marta Bergman who attended the Swedish Baptist Church, or the Schmidt twins who went to the German Congregational Church.

Andela and I talked the first Saturday night about our beliefs. With only small differences we decided we were agreeable enough to visit churches together and see if we could decide on one we both liked.

Andela's family's religious heritage was much deeper than mine and different from most of the other Bohemians, who had been raised Catholic. The Wersba family was Moravian, a group that traced its roots back to John Hus in the fifteenth century. But since there was no Moravian church in Sioux City, she looked to me for guidance. Our first visits were to Mayflower Congregational Church, the First Methodist-Episcopal Church and the First Christian Church.

I didn't want to go to Pilgrim Presbyterian. Lottie's comments on its popularity, and its large number of eligible bachelors didn't seem like the right reason to attend.

But one Sunday Lottie persuaded us to go with her---and since we'd tried several others and not found one we especially liked, we decided to give it a visit.

Pilgrim Presbyterian was a large church near downtown. There was, as with so many others in town, an ornateness that at once attracted me and yet repelled me. The churches I'd attended before coming to Sioux City had been simple structures with bare floors and plank walls. I had been taught that the building itself was not as important as the people who came to the services. But now on several prominent corners of Sioux City there stood elaborate churches I was sure I'd feel out of place in.

By the time we visited Pilgrim Presbyterian I was getting a little more brave about such places. But it would be a long time before I really felt at home.

I soon discovered that girls with motives like Lottie's were in the minority. Most of the young people who attended Pilgrim Presbyterian did so from purer motives. It simply happened that a number of male students from a nearby college were steadfast Presbyterians, as were some of our young women. It was pleasant to find a church with a number of persons our age. They even had a Presbyterian Young People's Union, a gathering of young college age and single working people. It almost could not be helped that Andela and I soon began to feel at home there.

The pastor at Pilgrim was Olan J. Kirby, a middle-aged man, tall and of muscular frame with receding brown hair and a large fatherly mustache.

When Reverend Kirby preached he enunciated his words in a stately fashion. His messages contained an urgency that compelled the listener to right living.

When he prayed his voice rose to a pitch as to convince one that God was hard of hearing. Reverend Kirby's grand passion was for practical living. That a man or woman should choose to live at odds with God was unthinkable to him. His messages bore out that such a course was folly.

Out of the pulpit Reverend Kirby was a simple man. He almost could pass for any of the well known Sioux City merchants. He loved having a good time, though never wavered from his true passion of helping people learn to live a right life.

Mrs. Kirby had died years before and their only son, Luke, was now in seminary in the South preparing to follow in his father's steps. From hearsay I soon understood that the young Kirby was a man of striking looks and great promise. Lottie set her sights on him immediately, sight unseen, scarcely able to contain herself until his visit home at Thanksgiving.

I could see why the many young men flocked to the church. Reverend Kirby provided a good fatherly example. He possessed a drive and direction about everything that the young men could look up to. But for me one of the most appealing things about Reverend Kirby was that he was a constant reader. He knew the works of some of my favorites---Thackeray, Dickens, and he introduced me to a new author---a Scot---George MacDonald, whose book, *Alec Forbes*, soon became a favorite of mine. I could scarcely wait to lend my copy to James Evans and to Martin.

When I wrote Martin of my decision to attend Pilgrim Presbyterian regularly he seemed satisfied, though I had long known he was not impressed by particular denominations. He said, "Just find a group who are concerned with loving one another with the love of God."

For the most part I found that true at Pilgrim. There was a good rich fellowship among us that was different from what I was used to when we lived on the prairie. There we had been bound not only by the spiritual bonds a church brings, but also by the fact we were all farmers; we fought the weather, the fires, the insects together. Plus, there had been but one church to choose from. Here in the city the bonds were different. Box socials were replaced by ice cream socials, weather rarely kept anyone home and the members were from many walks of life---merchants, students, doctors, politicians were all represented. There was a loss of the wonderful unity shared hardships and joys on the prairie bring. Yet at the same time I was learning so much about the world, meeting wonderful people who didn't even know what a thresher was but who could tell me how to decorate a parlor to the best advantage. I found more people who read the same authors as I did. The increasing influence of such people compensated for what might have been a loss of intimacy in other ways.

Some of the young women who had grown up in the city were aloof at first. They disdained the simplicity of the clothes Andela and I wore. To them anything homemade was inferior to store bought. They would have cringed at the thought of living several miles from a store. The city and its extravagance meant as much to them as the simple ways of the prairie did to me. I'm sure they felt sorry for me, but the feelings were certainly mutual. Though I enjoyed the benefits I was realizing from city life, they could never replace the simple joy birthed in my heart by the deep colors of a prairie sunset. Some city folk understood. They too had moved from a prairie home to the city. Most still held the same secret feeling in their heart toward life in the country.

There was one farm woman who did not feel this way. I suppose it's true that when hurt comes our way, we're likely to remember with regret the places where we were wounded.

Henrietta Madison was an older lady in the church, a widow who had once lived on a farm in northern Iowa with her husband and three sons. When their nearest neighbors, Jess and Lula Snow, died, their orphaned son Eben was taken in by the Madisons. Then five years before I came to the city an outbreak of scarlet fever took the lives of Carlton Madison and two older sons. Henrietta sold the farm and moved with her remaining son, Joseph, and Eben Snow to Sioux City. In those five years she had become so bound to the city that she was almost ashamed of her prairie past. The painful memories of farm life, the loss of her loved ones, and the lack of proper medical care, compelled her to urge Joseph and Eben to learn a city trade.

Eben was the elder and huskier of the two and found quick work at the docks. Andela and I grew to love him. Perhaps it was his quiet and careful ways. We both admired men whose physical strength was balanced with perfect humility. Eben loved Mrs. Madison, and Joseph was now his closest friend. But I could tell Eben's heart, like mine, was still on the prairie. He knew he was out of place in Sioux City---and looked it as well. To see Eben was to see a farmer. More than once his huge frame lent a clumsiness to his movements that embarrassed him. In Sioux City he was like a bird in a cage.

Joseph, on the other hand, accepted his mother's challenge to make a new life for himself in the city. He was blond, wiry and full of zeal for whatever he tried, which seemed to vary with the seasons. Once he had wanted to be a lawyer, but after a brief innocent illness, he decided to become a doctor. Later, he set his sights on a political career; and after one of Reverend Kirby's most passionate sermons Joseph was ready to enroll in seminary.

During our early months at Pilgrim, Joseph came under the spell of Roger Farnsworth, president of the young people's union. Roger was Sioux City's most promising young banker, and another choice target for the affections of Lottie Townsend who saw in Roger a wonderful prospect for a husband. She was eagerly joined by several other young women who also set their sights on that "handsome young financier." This brought to four the number of young men Lottie permitted on her list of suitable potential husbands. Even Mrs. Madison was won over, and highly encouraged Joseph's zeal in following Roger's path.

As our president, Roger was a capable leader. Yet it became clear to Andela and I that Roger's interest in church stemmed more from the prestige it offered his career than from a desire toward spiritual growth. He even remarked once that he'd been thinking that attending one of Sioux City's "high" churches might suit him better.

I didn't care for Roger, but I considered his presence at Pilgrim yet another opportunity to understand the different kinds of people in the world. And though Lottie's ways too were different, we enjoyed her immensely. She possessed a great sense of humor, something both Andela and I wished we could express more openly ourselves. As for Lottie's search for a man, Andela and I simply enjoyed Pilgrim without the added pressure of husband hunting. Andela and I had been strictly taught that young women ought to be sought by the correct man, not act as the seeker themselves.

In our rooms on Sunday evening we often laughed at the antics of the flirtatious young women at the Academy who vowed they'd *die* if they weren't engaged by graduation. Andela and I knew their goals were much shorter range than that. Several had no intention of graduating at all. It was a guessing game as to who'd be first to announce her engagement.

Within a few weeks of our joining Pilgrim, Andela and I were faced with an awkward situation. Andela actually, more than me. Young Farnsworth, who, rumor had it, had flattered many a young woman to the point of anticipating a ring, all at once seemed to set his sights on Andela.

Nothing could have dismayed her more.

His romantic intent began with innocent compliments which Andela received in equal innocence.

But when one Saturday a bouquet of flowers was delivered to the Academy, several of the young women gathered around Magda Schmidt who had signed for the delivery.

"Who are they for?" demanded Marian eagerly.

"Probably Rowena or Rose," said Joan Frimmer with resignation. "They're the only ones who seem to make *that* kind of impression with men rich enough to send flowers."

"No," Magda said, reading the name handsomely inscribed on the small envelope attached to the box. "These are for Andela."

"Andela? Who's Andela?" asked one of the seniors who had little regard for us new students.

"Andela Wersba," Magda said. With that the girls turned and rushed up to our room where Andela sat at her study table writing home.

I stood amused behind the girls as they opened the door without knocking and pushed the box into Andela's arms, giggling.

"Open the card," said Marian. A chorus of echoes urged her on.

"Who are they from?" someone begged.

Andela's complexion reddened as she slowly opened the tiny envelope.

When Andela, quite embarrassed, didn't speak, Lottie stepped up and took the card from her and read:

"To the fairest at Pilgrim
From your ardent admirer,
Roger Farnsworth."

Several voices gave out an envious sigh. I decided it was time to rescue Andela and said, "Okay, you've all had your thrill of the week, now be about your own business."

The girls turned and crowded out the door with a wave of gossip between them. The buzz of their voices continued down the stairs.

"They're pretty, Andela," I said, in sympathy, knowing immediately her feelings. "Let's put them in water."

"Ann, have I said anything to encourage Mr. Farnsworth?" Andela asked with hesitation.

39

"Of course not. You've done nothing to warrant these ...except being the wonderful person you are. I should think many a young man would wish to send you flowers.

"But I seek no such attention."

"I know. But I suspect one day, you'll welcome it. Though perhaps not from the heart of Roger Farnsworth."

"What shall I say at church tomorrow? I must stay at home!"

"No, Andela. We'll go, we'll sit together as always and when you see Roger you will simply say 'Thank you for the delightful flowers.' And let it go at that."

"How can I let him know I wish him to...not to show interest in me?"

"Well, from what we've heard, perhaps you should just weather it. No doubt this is another of his passing fancies. Next week it'll be someone else."

"I hope so."

But though Andela refused to do more than offer a simple thank you for Roger's good wishes, he continued to give her compliments and more attention than she wished.

Good natured Lottie soon understood the situation and teased Andela, not without some jealousy I was certain, on being the first to attract a man. "And what a catch he'd be!" she said, lamenting her own failure to do as well and wishing some of Roger's attentions would come her way.

The episode certainly added a good deal of spice to our church-going for a time!

These early days at the Academy were turning out to be so special. I was making friends and I was learning, studying every day, and hearing from my teachers of wonders I know some people, like my sister Elsie, could never understand or appreciate.

I could barely wait until the Thanksgiving holiday. I had so much to tell Mama and Martin. More than I could ever write in a letter.

CHAPTER 6
THANKSGIVING, 1896

As Thanksgiving approached, most of the girls made plans to go home. I was to leave on Tuesday and return on Sunday. My only reluctance was that Andela had to stay at the Academy. She couldn't afford such a short trip home now, and then again in three weeks for Christmas.

But sometimes seemingly unfavorable events come along that later prove providential. Such was the case that Thanksgiving. On the Saturday before Thanksgiving, snow flurries began. All of us expected a short pleasant snow, just the thing to usher in the winter holidays. By Monday, however, the flurries had turned to near blizzard conditions, and we all were preparing for disappointment. The weather continued through the Thanksgiving holiday and into Friday. None of us was able to go home, except the few girls who lived within a few miles of Sioux City. Catherine Bonacre's uncle urged her to stay at the academy as he had "previous plans."

As the weather worsened, Miss Button swung into action. Knowing we'd all be together for the holiday, on Monday she told Artemis to try to get through to Malon's, the large poultry concern on the edge of town. She instructed him to buy ten turkeys and, if there was time, to stop somewhere and get a load of corn. Then she issued orders to Milly to "prepare a feast." Milly was a wonderful cook and we had all grown to love her dearly.

She had been with the Academy since she was fourteen, brought in off the streets by Miss Button and virtually ordered to accept a position as assistant cook. As the story goes, Milly knew nothing about food, except how to eat it. But under the tutelage of Miss Button and Luwanda Sullivan, she had blossomed. A year or so later, Luwanda went back to her people and Milly, with an occasional hand from Artemis or one of the students, commandeered the kitchen with great expertise.

It was the Academy's policy for the young women not to work in the kitchen---it was thought to be a distraction from their academic work. But Miss Button had become so trusting of her students that she often looked the other way when one or more of us sneaked down to the kitchen to help Milly with the meal or the cleanup.

As soon as our studies were finished on Tuesday, we pitched in to help where we could. Andela and I gathered several other girls and formed a spur-of-the-moment entertainment committee. I pledged myself to write a brief skit. Others offered to sing or play music. Margaret Simpson vowed to recite Hamlet's soliloquy, an idea which made Lottie Townsend groan.

The release from our studies for this unexpected time of fun proved to be just the tonic for lesson-laden young women whose homesickness would have to wait until Christmas. How silly we were those few days! Rowena Gainesborough, Esther Freeman, and Mary Gates, clearly disapproved and walked away from our gaiety with their noses in the air. They cloistered themselves in their rooms to study, write letters, or read.

But when Thursday finally arrived and we were dressed for the hallowed meal, a strange kind of unity seemed to hang over us all. Perhaps it was the realization that for this, a traditional family day, we were all together. Therefore, for today at least, we *were* a family and should behave as such.

We stood waiting at the back of our chairs while Miss Button, at the table nearest the front, looked around the dining hall at all of us. Then she said in a warm voice,

"Perhaps for this special day we can all join hands and offer up to God a word of thanksgiving." She looked my way and, no doubt because of my engagement to Martin which I suppose made her and some of the others consider me more "spiritual" than they, she said, "Miss Bullard, will you please lead us to God's presence?"

My face reddened. I had never returned thanks for such a group. I felt embarrassed and yet at the same time honored to be called upon.

After a brief uncomfortable silence during which I gathered my thoughts and tried to become "religious", I simply relaxed and prayed.

"Our dear Heavenly Father
We thank Thee for Thy goodness to us,
for Thy tender mercies and great love,
for all Thy provision to us, Thy children,
and, dear Father, we beseech Thee for our loved ones
with whom are our hearts this day, protect them from
harm and keep them that we may be with them again
at the celebration of the birth of Thy son, our
Saviour Jesus Christ, in Whose Name we pray."

The girls all joined in a soft corporate "Amen" which seemed to waft gently to the very ears of God.

The meal was abundant. We ate hardy and enjoyed the most pleasant of conversations. Each table of young women seemed to be thoroughly blessed by both the fellowship and the food. Even the table where Catherine sat appeared at ease.

As the meal ended four appointed women cleared the tables while another six headed off to the kitchen to wash the dishes and put them away. We had tried to give Artemis and Milly the rest of the day off, but Milly would not leave her kitchen in the hands of others. Besides, neither she nor Artemis had another home to go to. So Milly "bossed" the girls around as a tease and there was much giggling and foolishness from the kitchen. Miss Button found it convenient to leave the dining

43

hall. Such nonsense, should it ever reach the ears of Dr. Sinclair would surely meet with reprimands for Miss Button.

When the final table was cleared and the last dish put tidily away, we adjourned to the parlor where Martin had waited that first day. It was a large room, yet with all of us gathered about the flaming fire, it was crowded. We saved an area in front of the hearth for our entertainment. Laura Davis acted as hostess, introducing first the talents of Marian Sharp who played a flute version of "Camptown Races."

I had asked that my skit come early. I couldn't bear to wait through the evening. I couldn't enjoy much else for my nervousness. So the four of us, Arnetta Fredricksen, Marjorie Hewes, Ellen Dover, and I, put on my short skit. It was supposed to be a melodrama. I had Marjorie playing a villain to Ellen as heroine, and Arnetta as her suitor the young hero. But I'm afraid it turned out rather a comedy. Everyone laughed when there were supposed to be tears---but I was just pleased at the good time we were all having.

After our skit I stepped to the back of the crowd and found a seat by the window, next to Andela. The girls in front sat on the floor, others on various chairs and sofas, while many stood. Catherine Bonacre sat uncharacteristically quiet on the floor. As I watched her, I thought how childish this woman usually was, as spoiled as a baby. But tonight, she seemed instead like an innocent child enthralled by a circus.

The surprise entertainment of the evening turned out to be a skit Lottie Townsend had schemed using our dear Milly. Milly was reluctant to do anything that was not "in her place" as she put it, but with Lottie's insistence, she finally agreed. I noticed, however, that Rowena and Esther and a few others left the room, their noses once again in the air.

The skit was a moving and funny scene which all of us recognized as coming from *Uncle Tom's Cabin*. It was daring for Lottie to brave this skit. From time to time I think every girl looked from the skit to the face of Miss Button for her reaction. She said nothing but we knew she enjoyed it. It would just be another "secret" which would never leave that room. We all laughed at Milly's performance, but it was laughter full of our love, and she knew it to be so. But when her part was through she quickly stepped back far out of sight, fearing she might have gone too far in being familiar with the "white folk." I was glad Artemis had retired for the evening after supper. He was firmly opposed to being a part of our goings on as it was "unbefittin' colored to be mixin'." It made me angry that such as Rowena and Esther furthered that notion by their absence.

Margaret gave her soliloquy, several read brief poems they had written for the occasion, a trio of the girls did a medley of popular songs, then led us in singing some of Stephen Foster's songs. My voice caught as did several others when we sang:

"There's where my heart is turning ever,
There's where the old folks stay.
All the world is sad and dreary.
Everywhere I roam
Oh, darkies how my heart grows weary
Far from the old folks at home."

Laura was ready to close the evening---all the scheduled entertainment was done. Yet I knew none of us in that room were sleepy---we were all savoring the embers of a perfect evening. She halted a moment, hesitant to dismiss us to our rooms. All at once from my side I heard shy Andela say, "Laura, if I may...I have something I wish to say. And something I wish us to do."

Laura looked to Miss Button who nodded. Laura then said, "Yes, Andela, please come up."

Andela said softly, as she wound her way to the front, "First, you must excuse me for just a moment." She then went into the hallway toward the kitchen, returning quickly with something in her hands which I

45

couldn't see.

She stood meekly for a moment in front of the group, her knees slightly wobbling, then said in as firm a voice as she could muster:

"We have a tradition in our community. I would like to share it with you."

She had kernels of popcorn in her hand which she now passed out, one to each girl. As soon as each had theirs, Andela continued:

"It's our belief that as we express to God our thanks for the things He has done in our lives, and confess it to others, He hears us and is pleased. We state our thanks for that which we are most grateful and toss a kernel on the hearth close to the fire. When it pops it is a sign to us that God has heard. It is of course superstition, but my people still see the wisdom of its practice."

She then turned and tossed her kernel to the brick hearth, near the flame, saying:

"For God's gift of art, I am tonight especially thankful." Then she wound her way back to my side.

For a moment all was silent. No one stirred. Then Miss Button soberly approached the fire, and looking at us dearly, said, "For another year of caring for the best young ladies in America, I am thankful." And her kernel was cast onto the hearth near the flame, just as we heard a brief pop from Andela's kernel.

Laura Davis followed with a thankfulness for her family far away in Marshalltown.

One by one each girl made her way to the hearth and spoke her thanksgiving, some in broken voices. Of all the girls present, only Catherine didn't participate. I was surprised she even stayed to listen. I thought she might leave when Rowena and Esther's little clan did.

I kept thinking of what I should say when my turn came. There was so much in my life I was thankful for ---Martin, the Academy, happiness. But finally as one of the last who ventured up to the fire, I simply said, "My wise grandmother once said that living is change, God meant it to be so. My wise fiance says that this life on earth is as a promise for that life which is yet to come. And youth, these years we are now blessed with, are our years of promise. I'm thankful tonight for life itself, for the changes it brings, for the promise it holds."

The last three or four girls followed me with their particular thanks, and then Milly crept up to the fire, again reluctant to intrude on our gathering. But she boldly tossed her kernel toward the fire and turned to us all saying, "I am thankful for love and the one who has shown me what it is. I am thankful for Miss Button."

Miss Button said nothing but closed her eyes in peace and smiled.

Laura knew now it was time to close. But reluctant to send us off to a melancholy night's sleep she rallied us all to sing a favorite of many in that room. And those who were from afar hummed along, their spirits joining with ours as we sang:

You ask what land I love the best,
Iowa, 'tis Iowa,
The fairest state of all the west,
Iowa, O! Iowa.
From yonder Mississippi's stream
To where Missouri's waters gleam,
O! fair it is as poet's dream,
Iowa, in Iowa.

I turned and looked out the window at the snow raging fierce, the wind blasting firm and then at the fire and the girls, many my friends now, and was thankful.

CHAPTER 7
DECEMBER, 1896

For the next several days a congenial atmosphere spread over the Academy. We had all been touched by the events and speeches around the Thanksgiving fire. That is, except for Rowena, Esther and their few snooty friends. They still walked around the school with an air of superiority that made Lottie Townsend furious.

For my part, the amiable tone was welcome. I wouldn't let a few troublemakers ruin it for me. When I came to Sioux City I had supposed the halls of the Academy would always be ringing with laughter and camaraderie. Was I in for a surprise! I should have realized eighty girls living together would occasionally make for some friction. But I was brought up with the idea that people who lived together must work together and believe in each other and not bicker and fight like banty hens. Even Papa preached it, though he didn't practice it very well. We girls had been punished when we fought amongst ourselves and we learned to respect each other and exercise self-control and patience. It soon became apparent that not all the families represented at the Academy were so trained.

Some girls seemed to attract trouble more readily than others. Catherine Bonacre continued to be a source of irritation. Rowena Gainesborough also left a trail of misery---usually among the first or second-year students. She and some of the other older students felt they had more rights than the rest of us, especially when it came to bathroom use and dining hall lines. They felt their age gave them status and that they should be served first. Lottie Townsend finally could contain her anger no longer, and decided to do something about it.

She swore all the Freshmen to secrecy as she started her campaign of vengeance. I never knew one person could have as much mischief in her as did Lottie. She carried out the usual simple pranks of loosening the salt shaker lids on the table where the older girls usually sat, and putting talcum powder in the tooth powder cans. But beyond that she was always on the lookout for more fiendish acts of retaliation.

One afternoon she set the grandfather clock in the hall back a half hour. The rest of us younger students knew her deed and thus we quietly sneaked to the dining hall and had our dinner and were eating our dessert when the older girls were just coming through the door.

Then, she conspired with Milly, who was still smarting over the older girls' prejudice, to serve leftover beans and rice to the first thirty in line and to bring out the chicken and dumplings for the rest of us.

That particular prank was reported to Miss Button, who, though sympathetic to our cause, had to mete out punishment. Milly was bound not to tell on Lottie, but rather than leaving Milly to bear the blame alone, Lottie confessed. For a whole week she had to sit alone at every meal.

That only made Lottie angrier. It began to seem like Lottie's presence at the Academy now had three objectives, and in order they were: make life miserable for the older girls; find a husband, and; if the time remaining permitted---get an education. To her this last was simply an added benefit.

So much of what went on at the Academy wasn't what I had expected. It was natural, I suppose, that the days of my doubt would come, and come they did.

The unexpected joy of our Thanksgiving party lasted for several days. But with the approach of Christmas, thoughts once again turned to home.

Sometimes during my studies, usually Business class, my mind began to wander. I tried to imagine what life would be like if I had chosen to stay in Stebbinsville and marry Martin immediately. After all, when Mama was my age she had been married for three years and given birth twice. Elsie at eighteen had been married and borne Davey. I began to wonder if I had made a mistake.

I realized I *did* miss those at home. I loved Miss Button but she wasn't Mama. Andela was the best friend I'd ever had my own age, but she wasn't Vina, Lucy, or Mae. Reverend Kirby was a fine preacher, but he wasn't Martin. Listening to his sermons on Sunday morning I would sometimes daydream and try to pretend it was Martin up there preaching to all those people. I knew how he would have made the sermon a little different, how he'd have added just a touch of humor to make his point stick without hurting.

Or I'd envision his little parsonage and how I'd have it arranged by now if I had stayed in Stebbinsville. I imagined the work I'd be doing, keeping a house for Martin, helping with his church duties and all. I imagined I'd have the time to read books of my own choice. I could have my Cooper, my Longfellow. And I could easily imagine doing without the castor oil of Mr. Rothchilde's Business class! Mama had shown me a little of how she had handled the hardware accounts. That was all the business that interested me.

Sometimes days would go by and I would get so caught up in my studies that I'd have little time to think about all I was missing. But then something would happen. Polly Morse would laugh just like Vina or Professor Hoffman would mention a book Mr. Evans and I had read. I'd even hear someone raise their voice and I'd think about Papa. The worst moments came when I'd get a letter from home that had news in it I hadn't heard, or maybe a note from Mae tucked in it telling me how much she missed me. Vina's notes made me particularly sad. Papa was often angry, she said. Once Papa had come into her room and practically yanked her out of bed at five in the morning to make his breakfast complaining about his "lazy family."

It hurt to think of myself off in the city getting a better education than anyone in the Bullard family ever had, while the rest of the family had to suffer such things. Maybe Elsie was right---just marry Martin, have a family, and become the sort of woman everyone expected.

To make matters worse, apart from Andela and Mrs. Whitely, scarcely a person at the Academy or at Pilgrim understood my goal to write. So, when asked if I was studying for a particular goal, I'd try to find some less-than-truthful answer, or at least only partly truthful. I'd say I needed an education to help my future husband or that maybe someday I'd teach---a possibility I had considered.

Before long, however, it seemed everyone at the Academy and at church knew of my writing aspirations, even knew of my journal, which I was careful to keep to myself. No one, not even Andela, was allowed to read it.

As the days of Christmas recess approached, and as Mama wrote me of plans for a big family dinner---and when I thought of listening to Martin's preaching once again, the doubts about my being in Sioux City deepened. Only now it was worse. If I had decided earlier, in October, not to stay at the Academy it might have been fairly easy to go home. Four girls had done just that. But now after three months I was used to the routine. And I liked it. I missed Mama, but if I moved back home, I would miss Miss Button. I would miss Andela. And perhaps I would even begin comparing Martin's sermons to Reverend Kirby's. I'd miss old Henrietta Madison and her son, Joseph, and Eben Snow, though he had probably said less than a hundred words the whole time I'd known him. I might even miss Roger Farnsworth, Rowena Gainesborough, and yes, even Catherine Bonacre.

51

As hard as it was to admit, I had two homes now. And I was afraid being home for Christmas would make me have to choose between them. If I saw Papa mistreat Vina just once or if Mama even hinted she needed me back home, if Martin just said one word...what would I do?

That last night before I was to catch the train home, I lay in bed and looked at the cracks in the ceiling above me. They were like a map, a map of a land I didn't know. I had watched them every night as I went to sleep, like a child trying to discern animal shapes from the clouds. Eventually those cracks in the ceiling became almost a security for me, just as though I was still a child in my mother's house.

The next morning was a hectic one as nearly fifty of us scrambled around trying to get ready for our various trips home.

As the trains were scheduled to leave throughout the day, each hour saw a group of girls gathering their bags, bidding the remaining ones good-bye, and boarding the horse-drawn cabs or railway cars bound for Burlington Station. Artemis spent the day helping the women with their baggage and making sure they were leaving on time to catch their trains.

Milly gave small teacakes to each of us to enjoy on our various journeys. Miss Button stood rather idly by the front door sending each off with a hearty hug and a "Merry Christmas."

Andela left before I did. Her trip was much farther. As she left she handed me a small gift wrapped package.

It was the unwritten policy of the Academy not to give presents. Many of the students lived on such small allowances that it invited strained budgets to feel as if one needed to remember the others with presents.

For that reason I hadn't managed to buy or make Andela anything, though I had wanted to.

"It's not much," she said. "But you have been very kind to me. I wanted you to have something. You may

52

open it now if you wish."

Inside the small package was a little tablet of paper and two pencils.

Again Andela said, "It's not much. But I supposed a writer could always find use for pencil and paper."

I nodded and gave Andela a hug. She then hurried downstairs to catch her ride, and as she left I knew immediately what present to give her.

I continued my packing, making sure I kept the pencils and tablet with me.

A few hours later, I sat on a crowded train headed for home. I ate Milly's teacake almost immediately. Then I pulled out the pencil and paper and wrote a poem for Andela. I would mail it as soon as I got to Stebbinsville. It would reach her in time for Christmas.

Somehow the words came easily and I wrote:

> *A woman's friend is a joy from above*
> *She gives to others her gift of love*
> *To know of my Andela, such a treasure*
> *For she shows Heaven's fullest measure.*
>
> *I wish her the love this Christmas Day*
> *Of the Boy child asleep in the hay.*
> *And hope that in God's timely plan*
> *This friendship, our lives will span.*

It seemed rather childish doggerel as I read it over. But Andela would love it, and it would show her how happy I was to have her friendship.

I tucked the poem away for the rest of the train ride. As I watched out the window I thought of my two homes, my two worlds, each filled with people I loved.

CHAPTER 8
CHRISTMAS 1896

The best memory of my arrival home was that Papa, of all people, was waiting for me at the station. Papa who had more than once allowed someone else to do his picking up for him---Papa, who was too busy to "fetch the womenfolk."

As I stepped down off the train into the cool night, he stood off to one side, gave a brief smile and said, "Your Ma will be glad to see you." He took my two small cases from me and walked to the buggy. "Martin would have come but ol' Porter's wife is dying. He said you'd understand." I noticed Papa limped only slightly. His cane tapped lightly on the wooden walk.

The ride home was silent. Papa had nothing to say to his wandering daughter. It was clear that my coming didn't call for as much excitment as I thought it might. As I looked around the town, the changes I saw were slight---the new bank building was up, Hornbuckle's livery stable seemed prosperous, and there was a new place to eat---Franny's Dining Hall. Papa saw me looking at it and said "Stay away. There's been some shady goings on about that place."

I saw one or two familiar faces. But it was dark and there were few people on the street. Papa said there were so many new people with unknown pasts coming into town that those who weren't in their homes by nightfall were suspect.

When the buggy pulled up to the house, I felt a turn in

my stomach---I *had* missed my family. I jumped off the buggy, very unwomanlike I thought, and bounded into the house. As usual I found Mama in the kitchen. We stood silent for a second, looking at each other, and then fell on each other's shoulders in tears. I looked around for Vina, Lucy, and Mae, but saw no one except Gloryanna, our tabby, curled up in front of the fire. She raised her head briefly, as if I'd just been gone for the day, and then resumed her nap.

Mama and I released our hug and I asked, "Where are the girls?"

Mama winked and said, pointing her eyes toward the closet of the parlor, "Oh, I expect they're about...somewhere."

I winked back and answered, "Oh well, if they're too busy to greet their loving sister. I guess I'll just hang my coat up and sit a spell." As I opened the door with a swift tug, three round faces with large smiles leaped toward me with a "BOO!" and then burst into peals of laughter.

Mae was soon hugging me around the waist as tight as she could. Lucy grabbed me around the neck and Vina stood by waiting, and after a moment said, "What are the boys like in Sioux City?"

We all laughed. I spent the rest of the evening answering the three girls' every question about their big-city college sister. After Mama insisted they be off to bed, she sat me down with a piece of pie and began her own questions, while Papa sat nearby pretending to read a copy of the Sioux City Journal I'd brought him. She wanted to know if I still liked it, if my grades were acceptable, if Miss Button was treating me right. They were all things I had written time and time again in letters but which she wanted to hear in person.

Finally, tired and talked out, I went to bed. My room was now Vina's, which she would share with me on my visits home. I undressed quietly, her rhythmic breathing filled the room. I glanced out the window and at the now leafless tree, and then beyond to the prairie. On

cold cloudless nights the prairie contains a bright stillness. The stars seem to be in league with the long
stretching land, as if they harbor a secret together
about the season at hand.

From downstairs the muffled sounds of Mama and
Papa wafted up through the stairwell. They were talking about me, no doubt. So often in the past I would
gather by the floor register and listen. Tonight the pleasant drone of their voices was more desirable than what
they were saying. Besides it would no doubt be immod-
est for me to hear them talk about me. If their words
were complimentary, I might become proud; if it was
cautionary, I might be discouraged.

I caught the sweet scent of Mama's newly baked pies.
I was home, I thought, as I lay on my back and looked at
the ceiling. For the briefest instant I was surprised that
my friendly cracks were gone, but then I remembered
they were in another room far away.

In the morning, I was to learn how things had
changed in the Bullard family.

Mama took me aside early and said, "Ann, I've got
some news that I couldn't write in a letter, I hope you
won't mind, but it's been a secret just between Papa,
Grandma, Elsie, Doc Matthews, and I."

"What is it, Mama?" I asked.

"Right after you left, only a week or two later, I discovered I was expecting another child..."

"Mama that's wonderful!"

"No Ann, what I'm trying to tell you is, I lost the
baby. In fact I barely knew I was expecting--I thought I
was just sick...until Doc called on me."

"Oh Mama!" I said. "You should have told me. I'd
have come right home."

"That's exactly why we didn't tell you. I don't want
anything to stop your education."

"But Mama, your health is more important to me
than school. You just work too hard---is that why you
lost the baby?"

"Doc says it's a combination of my age and other

56

things, perhaps partly my physical condition."

We were silent after that. I felt hurt for Mama and almost anger toward Papa. He put her through so much. It just wasn't fair.

Papa's health was much better. He had almost fully recovered from the accident at the Osceola County Fair when he was run over by a buggy trying to save little Davey. Papa's limp only proved he had defied the doctors who vowed he'd never walk again. Though Papa was proud about this, he was still unhappy about the move into town. Mama said that sometimes for days on end he would sullenly mope about the house finding fault with everyone. He missed his farm work.

Papa complained about the "inconvenience" of living in town, Mama said. There were no cows to milk. One had to depend on the milk man in his little white wagon to deliver milk every morning. There was no spring house in which to keep the milk. Papa had to buy an ice-box and Mama had to leave a card in the window when they wanted the iceman to stop. And in town no one had cream, except the little bit that came on "bought" milk, nor did anyone own a churn. They purchased the butter from the butter-and-egg man who visited them once a week. To Papa, it just didn't taste like the butter Mama made on the farm.

But what bothered Papa the most was that town people got up so late in the morning. And now Mama and the girls were following that lazy example. Papa had always been up by five o'clock or earlier, and the habit persisted. He thought anyone who wasn't up by five-thirty or six was a hopeless lout. Mama, on the other had, had no trouble staying in bed an extra hour.

When Papa had to sit around everyday, and wait until six or six-thirty for his breakfast, it was Mama who had to put up with his foul mood for the rest of the day.

The morning after I arrived, I woke to the sound of Mama's footsteps going down the stairs. I got up and went out to the landing and started down just as Papa said, "I swear if Ann hasn't learned to sleep in late like the rest of you. What are they teaching her at that school anyway?"

Mama just answered, "Sam, I'm going to have to teach you to make your own breakfast. Maybe that'll help you be fit for morning conversation."

I heard Papa say, "I didn't marry you to teach me anything, Molly. I married you to get my meals."

I returned to the room and dressed quickly. Vina roused herself and for a minute forgot about my return. She stared at me with a surprised look then said, "It's so good to have you home. We've missed you very much."

I thought of Papa downstairs and said, "Vina, is Papa making it hard for you?"

She was silent for a minute and then said, "Oh, Ann, since you left he's been worse than ever. It makes me want to find a boy like Elsie did."

"Vina! Don't you dare run off and marry just to escape Papa," I said.

As she rose to dress she said, "Why not? Every girl gets married sometime. I've decided to marry Gus Gruder or Don Matthews, whoever asks me first."

"Oh, Vina, it *can't* be that bad. You must not love either of them or you wouldn't say that."

"Well, I like both of them. And I'll marry whichever one asks me," she said with a smirk.

Tuesday night Kate Porter died. Martin had stayed with her till the end.

On Wednesday, Martin rode into town early and picked me up for a visit to the farms. Changes were happening there too. Since I had left, Cyrus Crump had died. Zeke Warner had married Lena Wayland and moved west to Oregon. By the time I came home in the spring what other changes would have occurred in my world? I wanted everything to stay the same. Yet how could it? I certainly didn't want to stay the same. I, too, wanted to see new places and meet new and interesting people. And I longed for the day when, as Mrs. Martin Pritchard, I would rock a cradle, tend my own stove, and help my husband serve our God.

We stopped first at the Stones. Hilda ran out to greet us with a smothering hug and, "Vat haz become of de gul gone to da zity? She haz returned a voman, ya?"

Ethan Stone mildly shook my hand as if not sure how to greet someone he used to sit on his lap. Little Katrina hung back, her two-year old memory straining to find a place for me. Hans, now five and freckled, remembered me, but preferred playing in the dirt to visiting.

Hilda was nearing forty and had also lost a baby recently, but she looked hardy now, though the tragedy had left a faint mark on her countenance.

We visited our old farm next, now owned by Uncle Phil. It's funny how the same house can change just by belonging to someone else. As I walked in the door, I could picture in my mind our family there on a cold February night. But as I looked again, we were gone and the furniture was Uncle Phil's and the pictures on the wall were of people I didn't know. Uncle Phil was glad to see us and proudly pointed out the changes he'd made. It was at that moment I knew I would be returning to the Academy after Christmas. Grandma's words echoed again, "Living is change. God meant it to be so."

As we rode off, I was silent. Martin reached over and put his arm around me.

"What's wrong?" he asked.

"Oh, nothing---that is...I don't know. Things change so fast." I had a tear in my eye and reached for my handkerchief as Martin stopped the buggy. He turned to me and said, "Now you know how I feel every time I call on your family...and you're not there."

I smiled and he reached over and kissed my cheek and clicked the horses into motion again. For most of the rest of the day we stopped in at Jed and Elsie's. Martin helped Jed in the barn while Elsie and I visited.

Little Davey was the most active little boy I had ever seen. It was easy to see how Grandma Dauber could be of great help to Elsie. Tracking him seemed to be a full time job. I saw at once why Elsie had begun to show that familiar worn face of the prairie wife.

CHAPTER 9
CHRISTMAS 1896

The last couple of days before Christmas had always been cleaning days at the Bullard house. Mama prided herself on having a spotless house every December 25. All the more so this year as Papa and Mama expected a houseful. Besides the immediate family, Jed, Elsie, and Davey would be there, Grandma Dauber, of course, Martin, and Ethan, Hilda, and Hans and Katrina Stone. And when Mama discovered that Mr. Plover, the man who had guided her decisions with Grandpa's money, would be eating alone, she insisted he come as well.

Mama supervised us girls as she made plans for the big meal, trying at the same time to keep the rest of the normal family life in stride. In years past, Papa had been able to bring a small cedar for a Christmas tree. But this year there weren't many available. The prairie, of course, had few trees in the first place. And the heavy snow around Thanksgiving had prevented many from being sent in by train. Still, Mae insisted we *must* have a Christmas tree. Mama thought it over and finally gave word to Papa that Mae was right---he'd have to find some kind of tree for the family to decorate. It turned out be be just the thing to help Papa get in the mood for the day. It gave him something to do besides check in at the hardware store and boss Don Matthews around, or whine around the house all day about how a "farm man in the city starts to turn to no more use than a woman."

The tree was to be a surprise for Mae. Mama insisted Papa find one and hide it until Christmas Eve when we would all decorate it and sing carols around it.

Vina, Lucy, and I had seen Papa perform many a great feat, but to find a green tree in December on the prairies of Iowa seemed to be asking too much from even him.

But so it was on Christmas Eve while Mae was in the kitchen soaking in the large wooden tub, the last of the family to have her Christmas bath, that Papa crept through the front door, and finding Mae out of sight, brought what he'd found into the parlor.

He went into the kitchen and pulled Mae gleefully from the tub and said, "Well, by ginger! While you were in the tub, I'll be switched if ole St. Nick didn't swing right on by the front porch and deposit on our doorstep the very thing you've been wanting."

Mae's eyes lit up. "You mean..."

"Yep, sure as your Mama makes the best pies in Iowa, there sits our tree." By now little Mae had wriggled loose from Papa and ran stark naked into the parlor and stood speechless before a scrawny four-foot green-ish speciman. Where Papa'd found that tree I never knew, and he would never say. But little Mae asked no questions. Her eyes widened as she took it in. It begged to be decorated.

Mae's eyes widened at the sight. "Oh, Papa!" she cried. "It's so fine! May we decorate it?"

Papa smiled and glanced around the room and said, "As soon as you return looking decent, young woman."

At that Mae realized her state. All at once seeing Martin, who had arrived only moments before, she shrieked and took her small body back into the kitchen as fast as her feet could carry her.

We all laughed. When she returned in a few minutes her face was still beet red. But as soon as she saw Papa's tree again, she regained her excitement and Mama handed her the first decoration, a handcrafted angel made by Grandma Dauber. Then Mama presented a box full of decorations she had made or gathered. Cut paper dolls, hand carved animals, brightly colored paper creations were eagerly taken up by willing hands and placed carefully on the sparse branches of the tree while Martin started the singing with a boisterous "Joy to the World."

Papa and Mama sat aside and watched, threading popcorn chains. The decorating went on as long as there was something more to hang on the tree. The singing continued long after, until finally Mama admonished Lucy and Mae to bed with, "We've a busy time tomorrow. And...St. Nick won't come back till you're sound asleep." Lucy looked at Mama and winked knowingly, but trudged off to bed with Mae. Vina, happy to be included with the adults to stay up for a while, soon drifted off to sleep as she lay on the floor listening to the grown-ups talk. Grandma Dauber recollected her early Christmases with Grandpa, every once in a while Mama nodded and said, "Oh, I remember that." Then Papa recalled his childhood in Georgia.

We all went to bed that night with our own personal excitement about the day to come. The children with the gaiety of new presents and the tree, Mama with her lavish meal to hostess, and I to see my friends in our little country church. I was glad Mama and Papa chose to make the journey out there, rather than to attend the more convenient Congregational Church in town. Mama and Papa felt something special in Martin, just as I did.

During the night a slight snow fell---not enough to warrant the cutter or the bobsled, but enough to make us feel that it really was Christmas. We awoke to the sounds and smells of Mama in the kitchen. She arose just after five to begin her many preparations. She would be baking perhaps a dozen different varieties of cookies, she would have the plum pudding to attend to, the goose to dress, and of course several pies to ready for the oven. I had tried to get her to bake them the day but Mama felt Christmas pies should be baked on Christmas.

By about six-thirty the house came alive with the younger girls scurrying down the stairs and kneeling around the Christmas tree. Each was allowed to open one of their three or four presents; the others would wait until after church.

Vina, Lucy, and Mae each chose Papa's present first. Vina was given a knife with two blades on it for which she had to muster up some excitement. Lucy and Mae each were given small packets of store-bought candy which Mama forbade them to sample until after breakfast. When they were through we all heartily dug into the beginning of what would seem like an endless round of eating all day.

By the time Papa had harnessed the horses to the wagon, Mama and the rest of us were eager for the ride to church. We picked up Grandma Dauber at her cottage and headed out of town to the strains of "Hark the Herald Angels Sing."

The sky was now clear and blue. The light snow lay sprinkled on the ground like wafers of doily. The crisp chill in the air made us huddle closer to the hot bricks that lay beneath the blankets, and nearer to each other. I imagined we must have appeared as kittens napping in a furry bundle.

The church service began with the singing of yet more carols. Then the children from the nearby farms, many of whom I didn't know, put on the traditional Christmas play. As they began, under the direction of Mrs. McCavity, Martin took a seat beside me and whispered, "Mrs. McCavity's in charge because the pastor of this poor church is single. But when he finds a wife, this is the kind of chore she'll inherit."

I leaned back to him and said, "Then she certainly best be an educated woman. Not just anyone can direct such temperamental artists as children."

Nora Phillips, who was Mrs. McCavity's assistant had conceived the idea of a moving star reflected on the ceiling with a hand mirror. Joshua Bridges was the proud bearer of the hidden mirror. All went well at first, except for a few missed lines, ably cued by Nora. But when Joshua dropped the mirror, the Bethlehem star became a comet, plummeting to earth with a crash of broken glass.

After the service most families were eager to get home to private festivities. Soon we were hurrying home across the silver blue landscape, Mama visibly worrying that she hadn't time enough to do everything before the three o'clock dinner.

She needn't have worried. Grandma, Elsie, Hilda, Vina, and I were able helpers. We took turns at the plum pudding, mashing the potatoes, chopping vegetables, minding the pies, setting the tables. And as we all sat down to eat nothing seemed lacking. Even Gloryanna savagely devoured the goose heart with holiday zeal.

After dinner, much to the little ones impatient delight, we opened the remaining gifts. Christmas morning had simply been too busy for the ritual of all the presents. Mama stressed that waiting until evening was a good exercise in patience, reminding us of the scripture, "It's more blessed to give than to receive." The presents were simple, times being such as they were, handcrafted wares from the many talented fingers of those gathered. Each of my sisters had tatted new collars for my blouses. I told them how fine they'd look at the Academy and each girl beamed with pride. Hilda Stone, who had been her jovial self all day, from her delight over Papa's tree, to her third helping of goose, had made the most impressive gift for her Ethan. It was a coat, tightly woven in bright colors which embarrassed Ethan as he opened it. He reluctantly held it up and good-naturedly said, "Now where in tarnation do you expect me to wear this thing, woman?"

Hilda answered, "You vear it verever you be cold." The room broke out in laughter. We knew Ethan's health would face worse dangers than the cold of night if he refused to wear it.

Martin gave me a blue and white cameo. It was the most beautiful one I'd ever seen.

But the present which was perhaps the most memorable, especially to Vina and I, was the small pony Papa gave Davey. He brought it around to the front porch as the last presentation of the day, then took us all outside to show us what turned out to be a surprise---even to Mama.

Papa announced bravely, "I once gave mounts to Ann and Vina." He didn't mention that in a fit of rage he had also given them away without our knowledge. I looked at Vina as Papa placed Davey on the back of "hursey" as Davey called him. She, like me, hid well the stab of pain that lingered over the loss of what had been the dearest gift we had ever received. Lucy and Mae looked at their packets of candy with a little less enthusiasm than they had only hours earlier. Each child present was then given a lengthy ride on "hursey."

Hans and Katrina Stone squealed with ecstasy as Papa set them on the pony's back. Little Hans was just like Davey, full of prime vinegar. Once the horse started to move, Katrina gave a quick glance of fear, but then eased back and enjoyed her ride. Vina and I took charge of cleaning up after the meal while the others relaxed.

All too soon the day ended. The celebration was over. We all went to bed early that night, after bidding farewells to Jed and Elsie, the Stones, Mr. Plover, and my Martin. I watched him ride off down Main Street in his buggy until he was out of sight.

I turned back to the house feeling a sharp chill almost at the very moment when, like the night before, small white flakes began falling from the dark sky.

Later I came to savor that Christmas in my memory, for it was to be the last such family Christmas when all of us would be together. Had I known then how events would change our lives in the next months and years I would have appreciated even more those yuletide days of 1896.

The snow that began to fall that Christmas night continued for several days. December 28 was to have been a festive one in Stebbinsville, marking the fiftieth anniversary of Iowa's statehood. But speeches had to be cancelled and potlucks postponed on account of the weather. But as the Christmas festivities were so recently past, many people, I think Mama included, were silently relieved.

I was to be back in Sioux City for class Monday, January 4. As year's end approached, I wondered if once again in so short a time my travel plans would have to be changed on account of the weather.

On New Year's Eve I had planned to ride out to be with Martin for the traditional Watch-night service. That too was laid astray by the snow. So the Bullard family sat home to bring in 1897 by themselves. Mama had promised Lucy and Mae they could stay up to usher in the year, as would Vina and I, but, as she no doubt knew they would, they fell fast asleep long before midnight, and Papa then carried them up to bed. I watched as he grimaced in short stabs of pain. I would have offered to help, but knew better. Carrying his girls to bed was one of the few ways he could show his concern for his daughters without having to tell them he loved them. Vina, also unable to remain awake, staggered up the steps by herself.

I left Stebbinsville and that last wonderful Christmas behind me when I boarded the train on Saturday. The snow had stopped but we were advised the tracks might not be clear all the way to Sioux City and indeed they weren't. The ride proved many hours longer than usual from snowdrift after snowdrift, each of which had to be manually shoveled away by the crew and some of the more able-bodied passengers.

My consolation was having Dickens' *David Copperfield* to keep me company. I not only finished the first reading but out of boredom started reading it through again. It took my mind off the terrible cold drafts that blew through my railway car and made me feel less conspicuous as a woman traveling alone.

Martin had offered to come---he really wanted to, but I knew his place was in the pulpit the next morning. I would have to get used to sharing the man I loved with the sheep who were in his care. We simply kissed gently goodbye at the station as the conductor called, "Board!"

Many hours later the train jerked lazily into the Sioux City station and I was roused from what had been a lengthy nap. I had dreamed of James and Julia Evans. My one regret of the Christmas season had been their decision to spend it visiting in St. Louis. If we could only have know how long it would be before we would meet again.

CHAPTER 10
WINTER 1897

Before I had gone home for Christmas, I wondered if those who knew me best would see a change in me. No one said as much. But I knew they did, even if they said nothing. I used to think of myself as one of Mama and Papa's children, just like Vina and Lucy and Mae. But over Christmas I felt more like a full adult, like Mama and Papa. I no longer yearned for the romps I had enjoyed with my little sisters. Now I preferred to sit and drink tea and exchange ideas and news. I knew I was becoming a woman, and that was what mattered. I finally knew that I made the right choice in enrolling in the Academy.

The early months of 1897 found me much in study, and much in writing. Mrs. Whitely seemed convinced that I musn't suffer her unpublished fate. She asked me to do several "nuggets" as she described them. They were short pieces, usually long on character, short on plot. She was determined for me to understand the importance of creating believable characters. At first I sent these nuggets to Martin to read after Mrs. Whitely had finished them. I had hoped Martin would see, through my writing, how important becoming an author was to me. The reply from him after my sending my first two pieces was an indication of what lay ahead. I eagerly grasped the letter waiting for his verdict on my precious work, only to read his lines of news about home. Then at the close of the letter, he simply said, "So, this is what you write. It sounds quite fine to me." I sat down on the edge of the bed, and read the letter again. I loved Martin. He meant all to me---yet writing was becoming increasingly my second great love---oh, that he couldn't share the passion of it, that he couldn't give me more encouragement. Soon I no longer sent him my nuggets, but simply filed them away in a box in my closet, only occasionally pulling them out to re-read myself. Each character had, through Mrs. Whitely's exhortation, become real to me.

As an artist, Andela was slightly more appreciative than Martin. But her interests were visual, not literary. How I longed for a sympathetic heart beyond Mrs. Whitely's.

Once I tried to show something I'd written to Professor Hoffman. I respected his literary opinion even more than Mrs. Whitely's. One weekend he took a series of nuggets I had written home to read. I sensed an impatience about his agreeing to, which embarrassed me. Perhaps I shouldn't have imposed, I thought.

The Saturday and Sunday of that weekend proved extremely long. I wished so hard for Monday to come when, I imagined, I'd walk into Professor Hoffman's class and he'd say to the whole class something like--- "Young ladies, today we're taking a brief respite from our look at the work of Samuel Johnson to consider a sampling of a much more modern and interesting writer. One, in fact, whom I believe may be America's next Louisa May Alcott." Then Professor Hoffman would walk slowly over to my desk and standing behind me, he'd put his hands on my shoulders and say, "Young ladies, based on some brief sketches I've just read this weekend, I believe the name Ann Bullard will be one long remembered in the annals of American literature." My face would be red with embarrassment, my heart beating with joy over the acknowledgement of my talent.

I began that weekend to outline the plot for my first novel. I decided it would be a sweeping saga. With pen and paper neatly arranged at my small desk, I sat all

Sunday afternoon, inventing a whole new set of characters and outlining what would be the great Civil War novel.

Andela watched me for a while from where she lay in her bed reading. Then she asked, "Letters to home, Ann?"

Reluctant to tell all at first, I simply said, "No, I'm experimenting."

She pressed me further. "About what?"

I set my pen down and turned to face Andela with a smile, "Professor Hoffman is reading some of my best nuggets this weekend," I said. "He just *has* to like them!"

Andela had a gentle look on her face. "I'm sure he will." Then she added, "And what are you writing now?"

"More nuggets---only this time I'm going to figure out how to put them into a plot."

"A book? You're beginning a book?"

Sheepishly I nodded, then said, "Miss Alcott sold her first story at sixteen!"

Andela came over to the desk and put her arm around me. "Just remember," she said, "many of my early paintings were quite bad. I'm sure in writing too, it takes time and practice before a masterpiece is produced."

"Yes that's true," I said, but secretly I was sure I'd be different. After all, if Miss Alcott sold a story at sixteen, well, I was a full two years older than that.

Monday morning passed very slowly. I saw Professor Hoffman once or twice, assuming he'd wait until class to discuss my work.

But my literature class came and went without a word about my writing. Then I realized he was taking his time with it, not wanting to rush. After all, it was nearly twenty hand-written pages.

So on Tuesday, I again waited through a long morning.

On Wednesday Andela suggested I simply ask Mr.

Hoffman, rather than waiting impatiently any longer. I was barely able to eat my meals or sleep a full night.

So when, after Thursday's class he still hadn't returned my nuggets, I went up to his desk after class, like a puppy with its tail between its legs. He was busy preparing an exam for another class, and for a few seconds didn't notice me.

Finally though, he said, "Yes, Miss Bullard, you wanted something?"

"My nuggets...sir..you have them?"

"Your what?"

"I mean my characters that I wrote out for you to look at. I gave them to you last Friday...to read."

He looked up from his papers. "Yes, certainly. I have them right here in my drawer."

"And?" I asked daringly.

"And what? I've given them a cursory look. They seem adequate to me."

"Adequate, sir?"

"Yes, I assume they're an exercise for perhaps Mrs. Whitely's class, or some such?"

"Well, rather." I said. "But did you care for them? Did my Portland Sanders---the characters, the people...I mean, didn't Waverly Jones captivate you?" I blurted.

Professor Hoffman put his pen down with a slight snap on the desk. "Miss Bullard, I'm quite busy. Your Waverly Jones and all your characters, as much as I managed to read, were quite adequate, nothing more. Certainly so for a young woman such as yourself. But frankly, your Mr. Sanders is rather a bore as literary characters go. Certainly *you* know that. Why compared to the likes of say Miss Bronte's Heathcliff, well you've a very good distance to go, my dear. Now if you please, I really must carry on." He reached into his bottom drawer and pulled out the large brown envelope in which I had put my nuggets. He handed it to me with a pert, "Good day, Miss Bullard."

I picked up the envelope and headed slowly out the door. As I walked down the hall to my room I slit open

the envelope. It was still sealed. And Portland Sanders was a woman, not a man. Professor Hoffman hadn't even looked at my work. I pulled out the sheets I had labored on so hard, still unread. I wanted to cry but dared not. The hall was full of young women on their way to their rooms, their academic day ended. I could scarcely pay attention as I held back the tears. As I turned the corner to the hallway leading to my room I bumped into Marian Sharp and my papers floated to the floor, as did Marian's. I stood there motionless for a second unable to move or think. As the girls began to gather around, someone picked up my papers, and then I heard the voice of Esther Freeman and saw the attentive face of Rowena Gainesborough as Esther read---
" 'Oh, Portland, you must say you love me, or I die! Say it my love, and make me the happiest of men!' "

Catherine Bonacre's voice was now heard as she read the next lines, "His manly good looks and gentle humor were what first attracted Portland to Lt. Waverly Jones. He stood tall in his deep blue uniform. His gold buttons glistened in the sun, their reflection casting pure golden beams across her eyes."

Then I heard laughter and before I knew it I ran down the hall to my room, swung the door open and fell on the bed in tears.

I continued to hear jeers from down the hall as accentuated voices read my lines. It all sounded so awful. Not just the jeers but the way my words were being misread. I couldn't bear it. I wished I could be anywhere else---Oh, to escape the sound and feeling of utter humiliation!

In a few minutes, the voices stopped, and Marian Sharp entered without knocking, carrying my papers. Embarrassed too, she simply set the papers on the foot of my bed and left. I lay there a very long time. I knew then I'd never be a successful writer.

After a few minutes there was a knock on my door. When I didn't answer, the knob turned slowly and Lottie entered. I sat up on my bed, still crying. Lottie sat down beside me. She had never been so silent. She put her hand on my shoulder and held me close, almost rocking me gently for a few minutes.

"Lottie, I'm so embarrassed." I said.

"I know, I know. But you'll show 'em. One day your name *will* be on the cover of a book. I know it will. You'll show 'em. Don't give up."

The agony of that experience was almost worth the closeness I felt toward Lottie afterward. She didn't really understand my writing desires any more than my sister Elsie did. But she was willing to stick up for me when others turned against me. That meant a lot.

Andela was in the parlor downstairs during this entire episode. When Lottie told her what had happened at dinner, Andela finished quickly and rushed up to the room to comfort me too. I stayed in my room through dinner, I wasn't hungry and especially wasn't prepared to face the teasing I was certain would make its way from table to table as somone would mimic the lines they'd heard in the hall.

Andela brought me my journal and made me write about it, the most humiliating day since Papa found Tom Simpson and I in the buffalo wallow the day I broke my leg. He had falsely accused me of impropriety. As much as that day stung in my memory, this one would certainly rival it for feelings of disgrace.

And as ardent as Lottie was in her assurance that someday I'd make them all sorry by being a writer, I had trouble believing it myself that night. I wept until I finally fell asleep.

CHAPTER 11
SPRING/SUMMER 1897

Other events that Spring conspired to put a halt to
my interest in writing. Mrs. Whitely repeatedly tried to
encourage me. She, Andela, and Lottie were my main-
stays of support. When she learned of my encounter
with Professor Hoffman, she said, "Oh, fiddle! What
does he know? We who teach are often the poorest of
judges, especially that man! Why he reads the likes of
Melville, a truly insane man if ever there was one."

I managed a smile, but reminded Mrs. Whitely of
Miss Alcott's sale of a story at age sixteen.

"Yes," she replied, "she sold a story at sixteen. But
her first novel...and most successful novel, *Little Wom-
en* came years later at age thirty-six---after much practice and much living of life; some of it in the harsh
realities of life as a Civil War nurse. You have time, my
dear, much time. These years are ones of practice and
apprenticeship. Good writing takes time."

The letters from home were newsy as always. But
those from the farms were far less frequent. Even Elsie
didn't have time to be writing letters. In late March her
daughter was born---Cora Lee Miller. Even with
Grandma Dauber helping her, time was given to the
work a farm wife always has---work I knew only too
well. How ironic that Elsie left home to marry Jed partly because Papa drove her so hard, and now she was
working just as hard on her own place as Mama ever
did.

The letters brought the usual good news---Gus Gruder had married Donna Elsworth, and a baby was already on the way. Elmer and Nora Phillips were expecting another child. But then there was the news that Tom and Nellie Simpson had picked up and moved on to Oregon, never to be seen again. Ed Bowers had gone to Missouri, and, saddest of all, a letter from James and Julia Evans announced that they were moving back East to New York.

Papa was going into the hardware store everyday. Don Matthews wanted to open a fix-it shop in town. So he had suggested that Papa might be feeling up to working his way back into the store. At first Papa balked. Once before he had tried his hand at being a merchant and failed. But now he decided to try again and with Mama's gentle hand invisibly guiding him, the store was prospering. Also Uncle Phil had turned our old farm over to his younger son who was marrying Minnie Ernster in the fall, so he moved into town. Uncle Phil was helping out at the hardware store by going out to the farms regularly and soliciting business. It was a stroke of genius to have two farmers in the hardware business. It showed the farmers that Bullard's Hardware was the farmer's best friend.

Letters from Vina continued to register her new unhappiness. Papa was always in a bad mood with her, especially when she came into the hardware store on Tuesdays and Fridays to help straighten merchandise. He kept an eagle eye on her and Don, and more than once accused them of making plans to run off like Elsie.

Of course, Vina soon took up that very notion. Who wouldn't think of running off the way Papa behaved. Who besides Mama, that is. Don, on the other hand, would never run off. It just wasn't his way. When the time was right, he would prefer to ask Papa for Vina's hand.

With Gus Gruder married, it seemed Vina would have to wait for Don. And Don would wait for Vina in keeping with Papa and Mama's wishes. After all, Vina was only fifteen. Deep down Papa and Mama both approved of Don. He spent quite a bit of time at the house. Papa still resented the way Jed had run off with Elsie, so he never let himself get close to his son-in-law. When Vina married Don perhaps Papa would finally get the son he always wanted.

By Spring, several more of the young women at the Academy were attending Pilgrim Presbyterian. Friendships were forming between Academy women and some of the available young men. Being engaged, I was able to watch these friendships take their course without emotional involvement. Roger's interest in Andela was long finished and she was too shy to consider romance. Marian Sharp was rather plain; the young men passed her by in favor of such as Polly, Margaret, and Lottie, who flitted from man to man like a spring butterfly on flowers. So Andela, Marian, and I stuck together at many church events, while most of the other girls paired off with young bachelors. Roger Farnsworth, Luke Kirby, and Joseph Madison continued to be the most sought after---yet each successfully eluded the grasp of those most interested.

The church's main social event of spring was the May Day Social, held in Grandview Park on Saturday.

The festivities were church-wide, with each age group having a different part of the day. The young children had a traditional May Pole. The older girls had a large garland they decorated with gathered flowers, and of course we young adults had a box social with the money gained from the selling of the young ladies lunches going to missions.

Miss Button, and Milly somewhat more reluctantly, allowed the young women to prepare their lunches in the Academy kitchen before the regular breakfasts were to be prepared. So at 4:00 in the morning, nearly twenty of us scurried about frying chicken and mixing potato salad. Andela, Marian, and I debated whether to go at all. We doubted anyone would bid on our lunches. But we decided it would be too fun a day to miss on that account. Besides if our lunches remained unsold, we'd just eat them ourselves.

The park was crowded when we arrived. The children were all excitement. Their squeals and laughter reminded me of soft spring days in Stebbinsville. I could picture Lucy and Mae in the midst of the fun.

Roger Farnsworth was already escorting a new girl at the church, Juanita Bowman, around the park.

The real fun began when the lunches began to be auctioned off. I guessed Berta Engstrom's would take the highest bid. But it was our own Laura Davis whose lunch went for a dollar. Andela and Marian ended up eating together as my lunch, to my great surprise, was bid on by Eben Snow. I had always liked quiet Eben and was happy to eat with him. Today he was rugged looking in his dark flannel shirt. He was the strongest, most physical person I knew. Yet his temperament was like that of a bright quiet child. As we went off to eat my lunch, I wondered how we'd ever arrange to keep a conversation going. We spread out a quilt I had brought and laid out the lunch. As I gave Eben his sandwich I asked, "Eben, what made you bid on my lunch?" And then I thought he might take that as a rebuff so I added, "Of course, I'm honored. I was just expecting to have to eat with Andela and Marian. I thought since I was engaged no one would care to bid."

Eben's brown eyes lit up. "I know about your engagement. He must be quite a fellow. I bid because you're a nice young woman and I thought I'd enjoy your company."

For a moment we ate quietly and then he added, "Most of the girls at Pilgrim are...are..." Poor Eben. I knew he was politely trying to say that they were sometimes flirtatious.

"Yes, I know what you mean, Eben."

"...I'm not too good a talker. So if I'm going to eat with someone I want it to be someone who is also quiet. And someone who won't be embarrassed to be seen with me."

"Eben, none of the girls would feel that way," I said.

77

But then I thought of a few who might, so I added, "and if they did it would be a reflection on them, not you."

I thought maybe I should talk about things that interested him, so I asked, "How is your work at the dock? I imagine some of the men who work there are rather coarse?"

Eben laughed. "Coarse? Yes, many of them are certainly that. But it's a fine job for me. I'm not trained at anything else besides farming. So I have no choice but to like my job. There are no farms here in Sioux City."

"Yes, I know you like farm life, as do I. But why do you stay here if you'd rather be on a farm?"

Eben was quiet for a minute watching the children nearby pulling a daisy chain along behind them. "I feel akin to Mrs. Madison and Joseph. And they don't take much to farm life. It's easier for me to get used to city life than for them to go back to farming."

"I've seen that you're close to the Madisons. I'm sure they appreciate your concern for them."

Eben looked a little embarrassed. "Mrs. Madison gets a little ornery at times. Joseph is a good man. I'm proud to say he's my friend. But since his Pa died some years back, he's been wanting some direction. If he was left to live with his Ma alone he'd stick with her for awhile---but the day would come when he'd light out for parts unknown, and like as not, never come back. That'd be a shame for both of them. Maybe I can keep that from happening."

For a while we just sat and took in the afternoon. The warm glow of the sun was a promise for the coming summer.

As we started to pick up our picnic we heard Roger and Juanita laughing earnestly from across the park.

"Tell me, Ann," Eben asked, "Roger Farnsworth is quite the lady's man. What is it the women really see in him? I don't mean to speak against him. I ask as one who would someday hope to attract a woman, and marry."

Before I could answer Eben said, "Forgive me, Ann.

That was wrong of me to ask. I'm afraid the pleasure of your company today has loosened my tongue."

I smiled and said, "No apology necessary. I take it as a compliment. I believe I've heard more from you today than in all the Sundays I've spoken to you at church. As for Roger, yes, certain girls find his confidence and charm desirable. But, Eben, you've got a charm that exceeds Roger's. You mustn't compare yourself to him. I'm sure there's a young woman destined to be your wife. It takes time."

I sounded so wise, yet how hard it was for me to take my own advice about patience.

"I hope whenever I meet her, that she'll remind me of you."

"Eben, you *are* bold today!" I teased. I knew it was hard for him to say such things, and I also knew he meant them. It touched me.

That night I told Andela about my day with Eben. She listened attentively but said nothing. As I lay in my bed that night I remembered that tree outside my room in Stebbinsville and how the lone leaf had floated to the ground. I thought to myself, "This leaf is going to be all right."

The next morning in church I watched the parishioners with fresh eyes.

Roger Farnsworth sat next to the Madisons today. Joseph was beginning soon as a teller at the bank where Roger worked. Joseph's interest in banking had finally resulted in Roger's intercession on his behalf when a position opened up. Even as the two sat side-by-side, I was strangely reminded of the Biblical parable about the sheep and the wolf. Joseph was so young and impressionable; Roger so grownup and successful in a worldly way. I wondered that Mrs. Madison could encourage Joseph to follow in Roger's path. Yet I knew it represented a security to her. All else had been taken away. Her remaining hope lay in Joseph's success.

Eben sat on the other side of Mrs. Madison. I saw him

glance over at Joseph twice. He knew his old influences on Joseph were waning and there was little he could do. With Mrs. Madison's approval, Joseph would become like Roger in a short time. To her, Eben had so much less to offer than Roger. His future held little to recommend it. I glanced over at Lottie, sitting with a new young man I didn't know. Her arm was linked to his securely. Would he be the one? Oh, Lottie, don't be in such a hurry, I wanted to say.

Andela was sitting next to me---I could feel a wave of melancholy from her. A melancholy that struck her from time to time as she considered her lack of confidence. I wanted to say to her, "Be strong, Bohemian girl. You are of much worth." I looked up at Reverend Kirby, this morning's sermon lost on me. I wished for one Sunday, just one, when I could stand up there, with knees trembling and preach my brand of sermon. Oh, but I'd need to have Papa and Martin and Vina and Elsie and Rowena and Professor Hoffman and certainly Catherine Bonacre present. They were among the ones I most wanted to speak to. On this Sunday in May I could declare I felt the rebirth of spring rushing through my veins.

But of course I could never preach from a pulpit. My sermons would be in the form of stories. As a writer, perhaps I could someday shout my feelings about the wonder of life, and people would listen.

After the service was over, I wanted nothing more than to hurry to my room and lay myself outstretched across my bed with my journal before me and pen in hand.

CHAPTER 12
SUMMER/FALL 1897

The end of my first year at the Academy came all too soon. After my earlier doubts, I had made it through just fine! Ten girls had quit. I almost had. But I managed to stay with it. I returned home, to my Stebbinsville home, that is, with a sense of achievement.

Although Mama and Papa had paid my way through my first year, from Grandpa Dauber's legacy, I hoped to earn some of my own money for next year by working in the hardware during the summer months.

I was able to put my growing business skills, thanks to Mr. Rothchilde, to use by taking over some of the bookwork from Mama. She seemed tired so much of the time. I begged her to stay home and rest.

Vina continued to help out some in the hardware, but mostly stayed at home and relieved Mama of some of the household chores. Papa still had a short fuse and, just like a Fourth of July firecracker, would go off with little notice. His anger continued to settle on Vina. He was harsh with all of us but just like he had once been prone to pick on Elsie, then me, now it was Vina, always the oldest girl living at home. And while I lived at home during those summer months, Papa seemed to recognize the changes of growth and treated me more like he now did Elsie.

Iowa summers are hot. Every dusk Martin would come by and take me for a long ride out on the prairie lanes I knew so well. The warm breeze came up and the smell of rough prairie would fill the air. During those long rides, Martin and I had a chance to talk of things in our lives we couldn't seem to express very well in letters. He'd tell me the sorrows of this family or that. It tore at him not to be all that a person needed to get through the rough bumps of life. I told him of how I'd be a preacher some day by writing my sermons in stories. He reminded me that that was just what Jesus did when He told His parables.

During the summer months I wrote Andela weekly. She was so glad to be home. She thought seriously of not returning to the Academy but I begged her to reconsider. I felt she would find something very special for her life if she would only wait it out. And of course her father concurred, reminding her that the farm would one day be Pavel's and unless she had a plan for a marriage soon, she better find a good education to help support her. I'm sure her father thought Andela's shy ways would create a spinster of her. The young men in Spillville were mostly Catholic and Hans Wersba put no stock in a future with a Catholic man. Better she go off to the City and find a proper "Christian young man."

Summer soon ended and so, too, the rides with Martin. I had earned enough in the hardware to pay for a good share of my tuition, but would still need some help from the inheritance. I told myself that it was only a loan, and someday when I sold stories, the first thing I'd do would be pay back the bank account that put me through the Academy.

I looked forward to my return to Sioux City. My only sadness came as I left Mama and Vina at the station. Mama looked so very tired. Vina cried openly. With me gone, Vina would need another shoulder to cry on. Yet even so, I was anxious to resume my education.

As the train lumbered south, the discouragement I had felt about my writing was but a distant memory, and I determined to write faithfully in my journal. Most of the girls returned except the ten who dropped out and, of course, twenty-two graduating seniors. It was a grand feeling to come back and not be one of the twenty-six incoming first-year students.

Miss Button was her usual spicy self as she welcomed us all back. Milly and Artemis were feuding over some unknown matter. Rowena Gainesborough and Esther Freeman were beginning their final year. Next Fall Rowena would be attending a law school in the East, if she could gain admittance. Few women did. Esther was planning a trip to France upon her graduation.

Andela was waiting in our room when I returned, Artemis behind me with my bags. It was so good to be with her again! As we ate dinner together in the dining hall, we joined Lottie Townsend and Marion Sharp in catching up on summer news. Most of Andela's story was reserved for me in the room. She was hesitant to speak of herself or her family in front of others---it was not the tradition of her people to do so.

But once alone, she told me more of her life in Spillville, and of her people than ever before. Her artist's keen sense of unspoken realities gave further strength to her vivid descriptions. Pavel was tall now, like a grown man. Yet the farm work was not good for him, she said. He must be sent to the Conservatory in Chicago. I read in her soft, warm eyes the concern she felt.

"I can't bear it when a great talent, like that of my brother's must be wasted," she said. "I fear he will die young, as the good so often do, and the world will not know the gift of his music. He is writing music now. He will be a great composer some day. Just like our Dvorak."

I sat in quiet contentment as Andela explained that Anton Dvorak was a popular Bohemian composer, a special hero to Spillville, as he had spent several months there in 1893. The Wersbas used to listen, with the rest of the town, as the great composer played the well-known Bohemian hymns, some of which had not been heard by the immigrants for many years. Often Pavel, then twelve, would steal away from the family and stand beneath the windows of the house where Dvorak stayed. Sometimes he would hear the master play. At times he would catch sight of the man as he came or went from the house. Yet other times, nothing would be seen or heard. Still the young Pavel sat leaning against the wall of the house, as a servant would by the door of his lord.

Since the great composer's visit, Pavel dreamed of nothing but his violin. He played it as though making music for the divine, just as Andela wielded her paints.

Yet Pavel continued to work the farm strenuously with his father. Though sympathetic, he could not send two children to school. And since Pavel would one day be the man to inherit the farmland, Andela was sent to the Academy in hopes she could learn enough to secure a good job until she could marry.

Andela had sold a few paintings in Sioux City and sent the money to Pavel with instructions for him to secret it away until there was enough to put to use.

More than once, Pavel used portions of the money to help his father purchase new farm equipment. Mr. and Mrs. Wersba were like children themselves, not mean-spirited, yet unable to see the purpose of furthering Pavel's musical talents. After all, he must grow to love the farm. It could feed him for life, a violin could not.

As the weeks began to go by, we settled into a routine. I noted that this year had a different tone to it than last year. Was it because it was no longer new? It reminded me of the difference between reading a Shakespeare sonnet and an Emily Dickenson poem. Both pleasurable, but different.

It was October when I received news from home that shook my world yet again. In late Summer, just before I left, a young man named Charles Stoddard had come to town to work on the railroad. His stay was to be brief, and we thought little of his presence. He was youngish, perhaps twenty, and strikingly handsome. He became the object of many a young woman's whispered speculation. He was lean, yet muscular and had a deep tan from the outside work required of him.

After work each day he dined at the Stebbins House. Rumor had it he occasionally dropped in at the tavern for a drink or two, and then headed up to his room.

I remember little else about my first impressions of him, other than that there was something about his looks and charm that while appealing, registered caution in my mind. I dismissed it as my imagination, yet now with this latest news I recalled it clearly.

Apparently Vina had caught his eye, and she had managed to walk by his work site on occasion. He had clearly caught her eye too. When Papa found out, he scolded Vina terribly and forbade her to leave the house for several days. Don Matthews also found out and, according to Martin, confronted Charles. But brave man that he was, he was no match for the rugged railroadman. Rather than engendering sympathy for Don, the fight, in Vina's mind, meant that Charles cared enough to fight for her. Thus, when a week later Charles left town, Vina went with him, leaving Mama a note telling of her love for Charles and saying that they were headed straight for Chicago where they would marry. She promised to remain an honorable woman until that time. Papa and Donald headed out after them immediately. But Charles and Vina had several hours' head start. Papa and Donald didn't find them in Chicago, though they searched for a week. They checked with the railroad company, but Charles hadn't worked out of Chicago and was unheard of there.

Mama soon got notes from Vina assuring her of her happiness and safety. They were "on the road" she said, but married and would be settling soon. Charles had not returned to his job with the railroad but had taken his wages and headed west for a new start.

By Thanksgiving Mama had a long letter from Vina in San Francisco. Charles was working in a hotel and received a room in partial wages.

Papa threatened to go to San Francisco and search

every hotel until he found her, but Mama said, "No, what's done's done. She's a married woman now." Then Mama added, "Charles isn't the one to blame." I began to receive letters from Vina too, full of a young bride's excitement. I wrote back offering only the best for Vina. I prayed she wouldn't be hurt.

Vina's departure was a blow to Mama. She'd seen Elsie run off and marry, I was away at school. And now Vina had made what most everyone thought was a terrible mistake. Lucy and Mae alone were left. And now Lucy, past twelve, was starting to notice boys. If Papa had his way I think he would have just as well locked her up till she was eighteen.

Martin said Donald Matthews was setting up his fix-it shop. He was sticking pretty much to himself these days. Like the rest of the town, he'd felt certain that he and Vina would marry someday, and her decision to leave had left him confused and hurt. Papa and Mama felt a great sympathy for him and continued to treat him with favor.

Though my sympathies were in Stebbinsville, and especially with Mama now, I turned my attention to my studies with vigor. This term my classes were Grammar, which I found quite boring, Mathematics for Everyday---a new class encouraging women to know simple calculations which would further their general knowledge. Much of it was repetitious of my Business class the previous year. I also took European History, another class in Deportment for Young Ladies, and a course in American Literature taught by Mr. Hoffman. I had no writing class at all this year.

Miss Button's lessons in deportment were required for every student for all four years. It was her contention that the way a woman carried herself spoke as clearly as her education. Andela and I were determined this year to be more diligent towards Miss Button's class. We wanted to please her. As most of the women, we dreaded her time worn accusations of committing a "shocking breach of decorum" in this endeavor.

In Mr. Hoffman's class, I turned from the English classics I had enjoyed so much, to the likes of Hawthorne and Twain, Melville and Irving. Emerson, I cared little for. Cooper I admired a great deal.

The school year fairly coasted along. Thanksgiving and Christmas were uneventful. With Vina away, and Jed and Elsie north in Minnesota to visit Jed's brother, the holidays were subdued, a contrast to the joys of last year. I think we all missed Vina immensely.

Papa and Uncle Phil were capably handling the hardware store with barely a spark between them. Papa's temperament seemed to have cooled. At Christmas I watched him nap by the fire. He was getting older. Lines deepened on his face. I felt in the presence of a good man who simply tried to do best by his family--- but often failed. He loved us, yet he knew so little how to express it. So out of fear for us, he kept a tight hand--- and the result was that we misunderstood his love. I wished a brighter future for Papa, but knew that the real key to his happiness would come when he would stop trying to be what he thought he should and just be the good man he was meant to be. Martin had tried to talk to Papa several times but whenever Papa sensed Martin getting too close, he would turn away. I hoped Martin could be like a son to Papa, since it was apparent Donald wouldn't be marrying into the family. I wondered if Papa would have held the same bitterness if little Benny, Mama and Papa's first born, hadn't died in infancy.

Vina's letters that fall were frequent and newsy. She was seeing a world none of us had ever seen. I feared for her. I still distrusted Charles Stoddard, but of course I never told Vina in our exchange of letters. I would not speak against the man she loved. At Christmas, she sent us all a fancy photograph she had had taken of the two of them. Charles was a hard worker, she said, and they were renting a small room right near the San Francisco Bay, or the "Golden Gate," as she called it.

I received a personal Christmas note from Vina

which told even more. She told about how expensive it was to live in San Francisco and in order to make do, she was taking in laundry for the well-to-do. She insisted I not tell Mama and Papa. To work hard for one's self was one thing, but for a woman, a wife, to hire out herself in such a way was unheard of. It spoke poorly of Charles Stoddard.

Right after Christmas, I received another letter from Vina. Charles had left for the Gold Rush in the Klondike of Alaska. When and if he made a "strike" he'd send for her. She hoped it would be by Spring. I felt sorry for her living alone in a city the size of San Francisco. But I knew her pride would never let her come home, even if Papa allowed it, which was doubtful at best.

The New Year came in with bitter cold---but no snow. The first two weeks were as cold as I'd seen. Artemis earned his pay twice-over by the attention he had to give to the coal furnace.

In February, the days started to warm. As international events were unfolding, particularly those in Cuba, we little realized how much America would change in the coming months---and the effect it would have on our own lives.

CHAPTER 13
SPRING 1898

The whole United States felt a surge of horror on February 15, when our battleship, the Maine, was sunk by the Spanish in the Cuban harbor. For several weeks afterward, the newspapers went on and on raising to a fever pitch the call for war against Spain.

In April, President McKinley called for volunteers. Several young men from Stebbinsville left their plows to pick up guns and join the cause. Among the first was Don Matthews. His fix-it shop was closed without a second thought, as he heeded the call. Others delayed their decisions, preferring to fight the war with their opinions which, according to Martin, were bandied about without regard. But when they saw that the call to arms was fashionable, many of them joined up too.

Still others, like Elsie's Jed and Elmer Phillips, were reluctant to leave their farms and their families. What good would it do to fight in a faraway war if your family went hungry and your farm sat wasting? Yet each let it be known that if their country urgently needed them they too would go.

Word from Julia Evans in New York was that James had taken a civilian position in the government to aid the war effort. I had anticipated hearing word from them of the expectancy of a child, but with each letter there was no such news.

Julia confided that they weren't happy in New York and until the war broke out, had been considering a move. But James' current position now made it impossible.

From San Francisco we heard from Vina that Charles had given up gold fever for war fever and was on board the Oregon, a battleship sailing down around South America and up to Cuba. Mama wanted to send Vina fare to come home, but Papa refused, saying she'd made her bed and she had to lie in it. Mama still sent her $100 from Grandpa's money to help with expenses.

The effect of the war at the Academy was small. There were tears when first one, then another, heard of brothers and beaus going off to war. Jane Hartley left the Academy for a weekend to rush home and marry her young man, not bearing for him to leave without her carrying his name.

Many of the young women saw the war as a distraction from marriage. They took President McKinley's call for young men as a personal assault on their futures. Esther Freeman was convinced that the President's good intentions would surely cause the death of the man, yet unknown to her, fated to be her husband. She would doubtless go to her grave a spinster as a result.

Andela sobbed bitterly into her pillow when the news came that Pavel had gone to Des Moines to join the Army.

"He will die, I know it!" she wept.

"Surely not," I answered cautiously. I knew from the stories of the great War Between the States that conflict did bring death. But Andela needed a comforting word.

During this time, Martin sent me a copy of a new book that was taking the nation by storm, entitled *In His Steps*. The great question the book posed was what would happen to this world if everyone began to walk like Jesus walked, if before speaking and acting, they asked themselves "What would Jesus do right now?" It was a worthy question, and all the more so as reports came back about the progress of the war.

As Martin was holding regular prayer times for the boys in war, so Reverend Kirby at Pilgrim Presbyterian urged the congregation to be steady in prayer.

Several of the men from our Young People's Union had gone off to fight. Those remaining were faithful to keep their comrades' names before the church in prayer. A feeling of care for those fighting remained uppermost in our minds.

Joseph Madison wanted to join the fight. His mother pleaded with him to stay home. She pointed to Roger Farnsworth's example--he would fight the war at home by helping keep America financially ready for battle. Such was the explanation Roger gave when asked why he didn't enlist. For once, however, Joseph followed Eben's example. The two enlisted together.

Since our picnic together the previous spring, I had developed a sisterly attachment to Eben. I sometimes wondered if he would have preferred a more romantic friendship, but he accepted my feelings with grace. He soon came to consider me as a dear friend; other than Joseph, one of the few he had.

Andela and I went to wish Eben and Joseph well the evening before they left. Mrs. Madison was scurrying about, a damp hankie dabbing at her eyes with one hand, the other packing food staples and whatever else she deemed necessary. No doubt most of these things were probably discarded when the men began their training. Joseph's excitement contrasted sharply with his mother's grief. He too was scurrying about, deciding which few possessions he would take.

Eben presented yet another mood as he sat stoically in his large brown chair.

We talked briefly, promised to write, spoke of the sorrow of separation. As we rose to go I said to Eben, "Please know that many people will be praying for you. We need you back at Pilgrim---it won't be the same without you."

Andela, who had been even more silent than usual all evening added, "May God protect you, Eben. I made

91

you this, if you'd like to carry it with you...a remembrance of your friends." To my surprise, she pulled out a small lace cross she'd made for him.

As he looked at her, a tear came to his eye. "Thank you, Andela. I'll keep it in my pocket, always, and I'll bring it home with me."

As we left, Andela turned to Eben and reached up to give him a kiss on the cheek. She then turned deep red. So did Eben.

We rode the streetcar home in silence. Each of us understood a little how loved ones must have felt when the Civil War had separated families. It was a sad, lonely feeling, but I knew I must hold it fast in my memory. Perhaps this was how my character Portland felt as Waverly left to join Sherman's troops.

At the Academy the war remained in the back of our minds the rest of the school year. Almost every woman had a relative or acquaintance in the fight. As reports came back of death, mostly due to yellow fever rather than battle wounds, each of us felt the loss as though we were one in spirit.

When anyone received a letter it was generally read and discussed at the supper tables.

Andela received little correspondence from Pavel and it worried her. That he was perhaps unable to write didn't pacify her. Each night she dropped to her knees by the side of her bed and pled with God to spare him. Often I joined her to say special prayers for Don Matthews, Joseph, and Eben. Eben tried to write regularly, addressing his letters to both Andela and me. He and Joseph had become separated when Eben's strength and work experience was needed in loading warships. Joseph was on the way to Cuba aboard such a ship. Each Sunday Mrs. Madison looked more and more distressed.

I wrote asking Martin to have his church pray for Eben and Joseph. He wrote back with an ideal way we could almost communicate with each other and pray for the men at the same time.

We agreed at precisely nine o'clock each night to say a prayer for our friends in the war. We took the verse that "if two...agree on anything, it shall be done for them," as meaning we could pray thus and have an extra assurance of answers.

The practice brought me closer to Martin than any previous experience. To know that as I directed my thoughts to Heaven, Martin was doing likewise made me feel I was almost a helper to him before our marriage. I also found myself praying for Papa at these times. Mama's letters told me he was doing fine at the hardware store but was still bitter about Vina. He had as good as decided that she was no longer his daughter, and he vowed to thrash young Stoddard should he ever set foot in Stebbinsville. I didn't approve of what Vina had done myself, but to cut her off seemed altogether harsh. I wrote her often, encouraging her as best I knew how. I could scarcely imagine what a sixteen year old wife of a soldier off to war must feel like, living alone in a city the size of San Francisco.

Catherine Bonacre was one of the few students with no one in the war. Her main interests were those that promoted herself. My natural feelings caused me to avoid her. But Andela's example in trying to be a friend to her, plus my memory of Martin once telling me how the best way to be rid of an enemy was to make them a friend, compelled me to try harder to be nice to her.

When she made fun of my writing that time in the hall, I felt like she had personally attacked me. Forgiving her was hard---but I was determined to work on it.

Now her cavalier attitude toward the war and the men who were dying was setting me on edge again.

One evening she sat at my table for dinner. Lottie had just gotten a letter from John, her current beau at Pilgrim, and had read it to us. Catherine was just sitting down when Lottie read the last paragraph.

"We want very much to come home to those we miss. There is constant sickness and occasional death. I

don't know of a single man who is happy in these
circumstances. I have even seen men cry."

Catherine interrupted with "Well, what does he expect! War is supposed to be unpleasant. Is he a coward?
Why doesn't he face the horror of death with bravery?"

Then she added to Lottie, "With his whining he is
sure to die. And if he lives, so much the worse. I hope
you won't marry the wheyface."

Lottie was the wrong person to speak to in such a
manner. Catherine's words had shocked us all, but Lottie rose to her feet and, red in the face, walked around to
the other side of the table and poured her iced tea over
Catherine's head. Every woman in the room was watching by now. Catherine jumped to her feet and slapped
Lottie on the cheek.

Before anyone could stop them, the two women were
on the floor fighting their own private battle. Andela
and I, as the nearest, tried to stop the fight, but it took
the small but powerful Milly, rushing out from the
kitchen to pull them apart. Catherine grew even more
furious now. "You get your ink stained devil hands off
me, you Zulu!" she cursed at Milly.

For a minute I thought Milly would take a turn at
Catherine. She started toward her momentarily, then
quieted and looked around the room at the nearly
hundred girls who stood in stunned silence. Milly,
humbled, shrank from the room to the kitchen again.

Order was restored. Catherine left the room just as
Miss Button entered. The situation was explained. And
Miss Button sighed and said she'd talk to Catherine.
The resignation in her voice made me wonder if we'd
seen the last of Catherine. But as Lottie had started the
actual fighting, both girls were given warnings and
restrictions to their rooms for the weekend.

The fight turned even more of the students against
Catherine. She had tried to make friends with the sen-
iors, but failed, and now they were about to graduate. If
Catherine returned in the Fall for her third year, there

94

wasn't a person in the Academy who would willingly room with her. Miss Button would have to match an incoming Freshman with Catherine each Fall. What a way to start off at the Academy!

Catherine seemed to enjoy allowing her anger at the world to be vented in the direction of those who might provoke the most reaction. Lottie was, of course, a prime target. Andela's temperamental opposite was targeted by Catherine too. She took fiendish delight in humiliating the most sensitive students.

A few days after her encounter with Lottie, Catherine approached a group of us studying in the parlor. She pulled a chair to the crowded table and tried to edge in between Andela and me. There was no room for her, but she pushed and finally said to Andela, loudly, "Move over, gypsy girl."

The room which had already been hushed in study, now grew even quieter as all eyes were on the pair. Andela tried to move over more, but when she couldn't, she said, "I'm sorry. There is no more room."

"No room?" Catherine said. "That's the way it always is, isn't it, gypsy? No room for Catherine. Never room for Catherine."

Andela smiled and rose, picking up her books and said, "Of course there's room. Please sit here. I can just as easily study in my room."

About that time Lottie got up from the table where she was studying, came over and said,

"Take back what you called her."

"What---gypsy? Why should I? That's what she is---a gypsy girl."

Andela didn't stay, she just said to Lottie, "Please, don't," and went upstairs.

Catherine sat down in Andela's seat with bravado at her victory. Lottie watched as Andela went upstairs. Then she heeded Andela's request and returned to her own seat.

I was so angry at Catherine I could no longer study, especially with her right beside me, so I gathered my papers and went upstairs to find Andela on her bed crying.

I sat down beside her.

"You mustn't let her get to you. She doesn't even know how to be civil," I said.

"Yes, I know. But it hurts to see her live in such anger. I feel so bad for her. And, even though she speaks out of place, the words still hurt. Ann, do the other girls think of me as a gypsy?'"

"Of course not," I said. "We all love you. You're the dearest girl at the Academy."

As she dried her tears she said, "The funny thing is, I'm really not a gypsy. They come from Romania usually, not Bohemia."

"There, it all goes to prove how little Catherine knows."

The next morning several of us protested Catherine's behavior to Miss Button.

"I know. Believe me, I do understand," she replied. "If there was anything I could do, I would. But Dr. Sinclair insists I look the other way. Not only is her uncle his friend, he's also prepared to leave most of his estate to the school upon his death due to his close association with Dr. Sinclair. So I've been firmly instructed to bear with Catherine until she graduates, something we'll all have to accept."

We left Miss Button's office in silence, the sentence having been pronounced.

In keeping with Martin's wisdom, I purposed to make the best of it. I would try to be friendlier to Catherine and perhaps gain her through kindness.

Spring led into Summer so quickly that year. Second term seemed to go by much faster than the first. Our classes drew to an end, and we all made preparations to return to our homes. I wanted Andela to come with me, a trip we had talked about for some time, but with Pavel's absence she felt she must rush back to Spillville. We all hoped fall would find the war's end and our young men home.

Ceremonies for graduation were held outside in the small garden lined grass patch adjacent to the Academy. The mayor spoke briefly, our Reverend Kirby gave the charge to the graduates, and with diplomas in hand, the twenty-six graduating women were given a standing ovation as they readied to step into their new varied roles. Rowena would be spending a month in Europe with Esther to the envy of most of the Academy women, before she was off to Law School in Boston.

Some of the seniors had been hard to live with. They paraded their seniority around like a holy banner that the rest of us should bow before. I resolved not to do that when I was a senior.

The same day, I boarded the train home. I was tired and hot, wishing I could be going home to Vina's humor and Mama in good health. The only pure joy I saw ahead was being with Martin again.

CHAPTER 14
SUMMER/FALL 1898

Summer brought the war to its height. People in Stebbinsville followed the news eagerly. Turnage Wilbursmith sold a great many Chronicles that summer. So brisk was his business that I boldly approached him about a job writing for the Chronicle for the summer.

When I entered his office he was sitting behind his desk speaking to a young man, obviously one of his reporters. When I entered he said, "That's all for now, Curtis. Just remember what I say."

Mr. Wilbursmith knew my parents but as he had come to town since my college days he hadn't yet met me.

He stood as I entered and said, "Good day ma'am. How can I help you? Classified ad? A subscription perhaps?"

I felt uneasy at once. "My name is Ann Bullard," I said, "of Bullard Hardware."

"Ah, yes!" he replied. "Your parents mentioned a daughter away at school."

"Yes, that's me. I'm halfway through the Sioux City Academy for Young Women."

Mr. Wilbursmith was paying me the courtesies one would expect as daughter of a prime advertiser. "How nice. And you're home for the summer?"

"Yes, and since my goal to write..." I began nervously, "I was wondering about the possibility of writing for you, that is, working for you as a reporter this summer."

His countenance stiffened. "Well, we are busy. Two papers a week now. But I don't think...."

"I'd be quite good. I'm sure."

"Well, yes, I'm sure you think you would," he said haltingly. "But a woman...?"

"Miss Alcott is a woman."

"Yes, but I have no openings for a writer of women's fiction. I want hard---pardon the expression---cold-blooded news stories. We haven't much in the way of a Society Page."

"If you'd just give me...."

"I'm sorry Miss Bullard. I simply have no openings on my staff."

"But..."

"And I am quite busy. Do give my regards to your fine parents."

I nodded and turned and left. I felt a streak of anger trying to rise in my breast. But I forced it from me.

So I worked yet another summer at the hardware store. But with every shelf I stocked, I vowed I'd someday be a writer, especally a newspaper reporter. I'd show Mr. Wilbursmith I could write as well as any man.

When I told Papa he just shrugged his shoulders and said, "Newspaper writing is best done by men. We understand a lot about life that passes a woman by."

Mama was sympathetic, but I could see her increasingly wishing I'd come back to Stebbinsville and settle down, though she'd never say so.

That summer brought us great tragedy from which I was able to see how unbearable sorrow can change a person for the rest of their life. At once I understood the bitterness of a woman like Henrietta Madison.

Just after the Fourth of July when spirits were at a pitch in Osceola County, we were in for a series of summer thunderstorms. For three or four days the skies rumbled like war cannons. Flashes of eerie light shot from the purple-dark skies. It was easy to see why early civilizations imagined God casting spears of lightning from the clouds. Everyone remained close to home until one day we awoke to a quiet, still morning. The whole county could scarcely believe the change. Were the fierce storms really past?

With some reluctance the townspeople resumed their duties. Business was brisk at Bullard Hardware as farmers, having assessed their damage, came into town for unexpected purchases.

Then, as suddenly as we had awakened to the sun that morning, we once again felt a change in the air, old timers knowing sooner than the young ones that trouble was on the way.

Wagons raced out of town under advancing darkness, women scooped their children in their arms and fled home.

We had had cyclones before, of course, but the urgency of the hour had never been as great. From confident sunshine earlier, we now huddled in our houses or storm cellars.

In less than an hour it was over. The mighty funneled wind had bypassed Stebbinsville. We thought all was well, not knowing the tragedy of the four farms that had been in the direct path of the angry force.

One of the four had been Jed and Elsie's with a barn lost and some damage to the house. Another was our old place now owned by Uncle Phil, which also sustained damage to the house. The McCarthys lost most of their corn crop when the wind sucked the stalks hungrily from the ground.

Yet the greatest tragedy was not in lost crops or mendable houses but in the fourth farm hit.

So suddenly had the demon come that Ethan and Hilda hadn't time to fetch in Hans and Katrina. The children had gone off to play in the compelling sunshine on the banks of Mercy Creek.

As soon as he saw the approaching trouble, Ethan hurried to the house calling for Hilda. Together they ran for the creek, yelling for Hans and Katrina. But as the force came closer Ethan saw the futility, the creek still being a distance away. He abruptly grabbed Hilda and pulled her, resisting, into the cellar where they waited in unequaled fear.

Minutes later it was over. They emerged cautiously and spirit broken, hardly daring to continue to the creek, but not daring not to.

Before walking twenty yards they came to the broken wind-tossed body of Hans. Katrina's body was found an hour later, nearly a quarter of a mile away.

It was the worst blow the whole county had suffered, Mama and I went out immediately, prepared to spend a couple of days, if necessary. Aunt Hilda had always been there for us in hard times, now we would stand by her and Ethan.

Grandma was needed to help at Jed and Elsie's, and took Lucy and Mae with her. Papa stayed in town to keep the store open. The newest catastrophe sent more business our way, business even Papa regretted having.

Martin preached at a brief funeral for Hans and Katrina. They were laid to rest in the small but growing Pioneer Cemetery located on the edge of Stebbinsville.

The change in Hilda was immediate and dramatic. Her once jovial ways gave way to near fatal silence. Her eyes grew gray. Her interest in everything ceased--- perhaps even life itself.

I returned to town right after the funeral, picking up Lucy and Mae on my way.

Mama stayed on for several days with Hilda, cooking meals, doing laundry, while Hilda sat on their porch and stared for hours at the distant prairie expanse.

Ethan's grief was no less felt, yet after the funeral he managed to pull himself together and busied himself with restoring the farm. He was just as silent as Hilda and seldon spoke either to Mama or Hilda.

Martin came to call after the funeral but Hilda refused to see him, and, a week after the tragedy, thanked Mama for coming, but asked her to leave.

There was nothing that could be done for Hilda. She turned visitors away, preferring her own silent prison. Mama grieved deeply for her and continued to take food out once or twice a week, leaving it on the porch when Hilda didn't answer the door. Ethan thanked Mama and said they both needed time---and to be left alone for awhile.

Mama was so affected by the tragedy, it robbed her strength too. But as the summer came to a close she realized her depressed state did no one any good, only harm.

When it came time for me to go back to Sioux City, Mama approached Papa one morning with an idea she had. As she served him his ham she said, "Sam, I've been thinking. It's two years Ann's been away at school and neither one of us has made the trip to Sioux City to see where Grandpa Dauber's money is going. I think we should accompany Ann back and see what her life is like there."

Papa was nearly half way through his slice of ham as he said, "Couldn't pick a worse time for it. Harvest is coming up. Farmers will be in and out of the hardware like bees in a hive."

"It would only have to be for a couple of days. Surely Phil can get by---and maybe he can get Jed to come in for a few hours to help."

"Jed's busy at his own place. No, I can't leave the store. Period."

Mama thought for a minute and then said, "Well, then Ann and I will sure miss your company."

Papa looked up at Mama and started to speak. "You don't think I'd allow..."

"Sam, I mean to go to Sioux City. I've worked steady and hard for a very long while, both here and for Hilda and Ethan. I want to get away for a few days and taking Ann to Sioux City is what I aim to do...period!"

Papa, now finished with his breakfast, got up from the table without a reply, grabbed his hat by the door and stormed out without a word.

Mama looked at me and smiled, "He'll cool off. But I meant what I said. I have this idea how the Academy looks, and I'd like to see how close to the truth I am."

"Mama, I can't wait to show you around. If you stay through Sunday, I want you to come to Pilgrim with me. I'll be wanting to show you off."

For the few days Mama would be gone it was arranged for Grandma Dauber to come to the house to help care for Lucy, Mae, and of course Papa.

Mama packed her bags and boarded the train with me on a warm Thursday. Martin had come into town to take us to the depot. Papa preferred to sulk at home.

The train ride was one of my most memorable times with Mama. We talked almost the whole trip. For the first time, I was able to show her my sometimes contradictory feelings about writing. It still was a passion, but in the light of a future with Martin it seemed so impossible, so insignificant.

"Sometimes," I said, "I wonder if I'm wasting my time at school. At other times, it seems so right. Then I feel like I'm keeping Martin waiting. Perhaps I shouldn't finish school. Maybe I should marry Martin right away. I suppose I could still write on the side."

Mama read the confusion in my face. I felt like a small girl again, needing a mother.

"Ann, listen to me. I love your father very much. But I was hardly more than a child when I married. I wish I had been a little older, a little wiser."

"But Mama," I said, "I am older. In a few weeks I'll be nineteen. When you were nineteen you'd already had Benny and Elsie---and were carrying me."

"Times are different, Ann. You've so many more opportunities. It's your grandfather's money that's helping you through the Academy. If he was here he'd want you to finish. So do I, and so does Martin. You're gaining a certain wisdom at the Academy, Ann, that I think you'd not have had otherwise."

"But Mama," I said, "You are your own worst evidence. You've got wisdom and you didn't have an education."

"But I'm also wise enough to know that if I had one,

things would be a lot different, a lot better. Ann, honey, these years are so awkward for you, I know. But there are greater years ahead. I promise."

Mama continued, "Ann, what about the young woman who left our home two years ago looking for knowledge, wanting to find out what made the world tick? Has she lost that zeal?"

I smiled at this woman I loved. "No, Mama. The zeal is there. I just have doubts about finding the kind of knowledge I seek in school." I motioned out the window to the small town the train was rumbling through, smaller even than Stebbinsville. "That's where the real knowledge is. There in every parlor, every kitchen, behind every plow being pushed by every weary farmer. It's in Chicago in the tall buildings where the people sit and make decisions that change the world. In Washington, D.C., where the President decides to send troops to fight wars, knowing he's sentencing some mother he'll never meet to a life of grief. And then women like Aunt Hilda. Her children dead too. The newspapers report more than one thousand dead from the war. Multiply Aunt Hilda by one thousand...oh, Mama, there's so much more to life! And then I sit in my class and listen to Miss Button tell me how to sit up straight and pour tea in the proper way."

Mama smiled. "I know it all seems so distant now, but finish school, Ann. Finish school. There is a knowledge that helps, and you're right, it won't come from the lips of Miss Button. But some of what she and the other teachers tell you, *will* matter. The things they say can be like dry cornstalks and it'll blaze high and warm some day and it'll be the knowledge you seek. But if you don't have those cornstalks gathered and ready for the spark, then when it does come there'll be no blast of flame, only a small and short puff of smoke."

"Oh, Mama, don't be so dramatic!"

Just then the train pulled into the familiar Burlington Station. To Mama's amazement, I confidently guided us through the maze of people, enlisted a porter to carry our baggage, and got us aboard the streetcar for the Academy within minutes.

I had alerted Miss Button to my mother's coming. There were a few empty rooms to be filled by late arriving students. Mama was given one of these to stay in during her visit.

The next day I behaved like a silly school girl showing off a new dress. I paraded Mama around town and introduced her to my friends and guided her on a tour of the city. I soon noticed, however, she was tired. I realized she was getting older and had seen so much hard work during her near forty years, especially considering her recent duties at Aunt Hilda's. Our shopping trip was cut short when Mama was tired out shortly after noon. She retired after supper. When I asked her if she felt all right, she said not to worry, that this was like a vacation for her, and she wanted to catch up on her rest before going back to Stebbinsville. She told me not to alter my plans---if I wanted to do something with my classmates, she'd understand. But of course I'd have my classmates the whole next year, I wanted to spend this time with Mama! So for two days we sat around the Academy and talked, read, and rested. I came to see that rest was the best thing for her and felt silly for thinking she'd want to gallivant around town.

Of all the women I wanted Mama to meet, Andela was the most important. But word came that Andela's father was seriously ill and she would be arriving back late. I was sure Mama and she would be kindred spirits. My great disappointment was eased when Mama suggested I bring Andela home for Thanksgiving or Christmas.

As the young women of the Academy returned, each had stories to tell of summer events. Usually those concerned the whereabouts of their soldiering young men. Lottie's young man, John, was in training in the same regiment as Don Matthews in San Francisco for duty in the Phillipines. Andela's brother, Pavel, was in Jacksonville, Florida, supposedly awaiting shipping out to Cuba.

Mama accompanied me to the morning service at Pilgrim on Sunday. Once again I showed her off to my friends. She remarked as we left, with a little twinkle in her eye, "Your Reverend Kirby is nice, but he's no Martin Pritchard."

Mama left for Stebbinsville on the train that afternoon. As I helped her board the train she said, "This trip has done me a world of good. You've made the right choice about your future by continuing at the Academy. I am proud of you, so very proud." There were tears forming in her eyes, and suddenly in mine, too.

I kissed her cheek gently and said, "Mama, having you all to myself for these past few days has been one of the best times of my life. I thank God you're my mother."

The train was starting its familiar rumble as the conductor climbed up the steps behind Mama.

"We're ready to roll ma'am."

I watched until the train was out of sight.

CHAPTER 15
FALL/WINTER 1898

A surprise awaited me for my third year at the Academy, one which would have a marked influence on my life. Mrs. Whitely noticed that several other young women who had come to the Academy recently, also had writing interests. The tide had turned from a year ago when my writing aspirations were thought foolish. Three women were interested strictly in journalism; one, besides myself, in fiction; and two were unsure of their writing directions. So Mrs. Whitely convinced Miss Button to start a small class once a week for the seven of us. Our teacher was to be a local reporter for the Journal, a Mr. Arliss Cooper.

The seven of us sat eagerly awaiting Mr. Cooper that first Friday of September. We envisioned a hardened, crusty old man with a cigar in his mouth. I had added the patronizing attitude I'd found in Turnage Wilbursmith in Stebbinsville to my image of the teacher and resigned myself to disregarding the person of Mr. Cooper and simply learning what I could from him.

How shocked we all were when Mr. Cooper walked into the classroom, a young handsome man with vibrant brown eyes and wavy dark hair. His ready smile put us at ease. Pert Lemly leaned over to me and said, "And no cigar, either!"

"Good day class, I'm Arliss Cooper," he began with a broad smile. "I trust you're all here to learn how to write. I'm not much of a lecturer so you might as well get used to thinking of this class as one long agony of cramped fingers.

"Take out a blank sheet of paper and write a 500 word news story on the sinking of the Maine using the best information you have." He then sat down with his morning Journal and started to read, as if oblivious to us.

None of us moved.

He looked up from his paper and said, "Well, what are you waiting for? A peace treaty to be signed? Let's pretend you're writing this for the Journal. Our deadline is normally four p.m., but for the sake of convenience let's say the deadline is ten-thirty, forty-five minutes from now. You young ladies are the star reporters and my boss, Ernest Thompson, is awaiting your front-page story. So get with it!" Then he turned back to his paper.

We all began to write immediately. I was glad to do so, relieved that Mr. Cooper hadn't made fun of us for wanting to be women reporters. The assignment was tough. When we were through, Mr. Cooper gave every one of us failing marks, pointing out mistakes we'd made and then constructing a story himself showing us the way it should be done.

It proved to be the first of many interesting weeks. I thanked Mrs. Whitely for her part in bringing Mr. Cooper to the Academy. She answered, "It's the best way I can think of to get you would-be authoresses on the ball. I wish I had had such a teacher in my younger years."

My other classes paled in comparison to Mr. Cooper's. And although two girls soon dropped the course, four more took their place as the word spread around the school about the attractive Arliss Cooper.

The first weeks were devoted to journalism. He brought news stories to class which he dissected for us and then had us rewrite. We were always told to think in terms of Mr. Townsend standing behind our backs watching as we wrote.

After the weeks of newspaper writing he taught us

what he knew about fiction writing, which was considerable. After class one day, I went up to him to thank him for the class.

"Happy to do it," he replied. "You know, Miss Bullard, you have great possiblities. You could be a good writer."

"Thank you," I replied. "It's been my desire, since I was a girl, to write. I keep a journal."

"Excellent! You know," he said slowly, "if you don't mind my saying so, you're quite a bright, attractive lady."

I reddened. "Well, I...I thank you for the compliment," I said, then turned and left. I wasn't used to such talk from anyone other than Martin.

Our assignments often had to do with the war. Certainly the stories the young women were hearing from their men-friends in letters and as the men began to return home were worthy of expression. Thus, one of our most memorable assignments was to take a story we'd heard about someone we knew in the war and fictionalize it. I knew several young soldiers, though I only heard from Eben occasionally. His news was never very exciting as his regiment hadn't even left the United States. But a few days before the assignment I received a letter from Vina which raised some possibilities. Don Matthews had called on her while he was training in San Francisco. He was embarrassed for her neighbors to see a young man other than her husband call on her, but she laughed and told him they were in San Francisco, not Stebbinsville.

Vina sounded so grown up in her letters. She said Don had called on her "to find out why she ran off and was she happy?" She told him, and me in the letter, that she'd done it because Charles offered her a future she thought she couldn't have in Iowa. She told Don she cared for him very much, but she was happy now as Mrs. Charles Stoddard. She hoped he could wish her well. After some refreshment he left and she gave him a kiss on the cheek for luck and old times' sake.

The way Vina described Donald as a "nice Iowa boy," made me realize how very much she had changed. So my story was entitled "The Nice Iowa Boy," and turned out getting me a very good grade and a recommendation from Mr. Cooper to send the story to some magazines to see if it could be published. Mr. Cooper's praise encouraged me to write more stories. I brought out all the nuggets I had written for Mrs. Whitely and gave them to him one Friday. I was in fear and trembling that he might react the way Mr. Hoffman had. But he welcomed them and returned them to me Monday with great approval, giving me suggestions on how to work them into actual stories.

Mr. Cooper's motto for fiction was "write from life" which was similar to what Mrs. Whitely kept saying. He encouraged me to create fresh characters from combinations of people I knew. One day he posed the question, "If you can think of a person who arouses anger in you, then if you can identify that quality in them that produces anger and successfully impart it to your own characters, you'll be a good writer." I started doing my nuggets again and found my characters providing their own plots. So absorbed was I in my writing, I found less time for my other classes. Andela and I were still taking Miss Button's Deportment Class and some of the ideas we were laughing at only two years ago were now starting to make sense.

I could see changes in Andela, not only in her deportment, but in many areas. She was as shy as ever, but now there was an appealing womanly maturity in her bashfulness. Her lack of social life gave her more time to study, as her grades showed. It was clear that she could graduate from the Academy and find a job almost anywhere.

Our friendship, always strong, was growing closer. Thus I was confused in October when Andela asked Miss Button to allow her to room with Catherine Bonacre, whose latest roommate had left the school after only a month.

110

Andela had always felt Catherine was mean for reasons none of us knew. She was determined to be a friend to Catherine and see if she couldn't help her. I admired Andela, but there were not two more opposite women in the Academy. Could even Andela's gentle temperament stand Catherine's constant complaining? I had made no progress in my feeble attempts to befriend her. I didn't want Andela to be hurt by Catherine. But Andela's decision had my reluctant admiration. I consoled myself with the knowledge I'd still be seeing Andela and eating meals with her every day.

My new roommate was Olive Randall, a second-year student from a farm in eastern Iowa. Olive was tall, wore glasses and was quite thin. She could easily have given the impression of following Rowena's example and going into law, but instead planned to return to her small community as a teacher. Olive was quiet and more studious than any other student at the Academy. I sensed learning was the same passion for her that writing was for me. She thrived on uncovering new ideas, facts, and historical knowledge. As I got to know her I thought to myself she wouldn't be happy teaching in a small community very long. Someday she'd be wanting to go to a University and continue her study.

Although I couldn't put my finger on it, something about Olive troubled me. It was as though what I saw in her was not what she really was. Andela said it was just my writer's imagination. There was really nothing outward to give any cause for alarm.

Our room was usually very quiet. I was either reading or writing in my journal while Olive studied. Gone were the days when Andela and I would lie across our beds and dream about the future, about having families and finding our missions in the world. I missed that very much.

Another thing I missed was Rowena Gainesborough. While she was at the Academy she and I never had much in common. She found me simple and unchallenging. At that time several of us who were friends didn't

111

think much of Rowena's ways, but now that she had gone to law school in Boston and Esther Freeman was working in a local accounting firm, I found I missed them. I liked having the people who entered the stage of my life's play to stay there. From time to time I found myself thinking of others who had been close to me and left my stage, so to speak. Tom Simpson was off somewhere in Oregon, the Evanses were living in New York. I even wondered about the few girls who had left the Academy after only a year or two. What were their lives like now? I had a deepening curiosity about those who went on with their living without me.

Most serious of these speculations had to do with Vina. I was closer to her than any of my other sisters. And with her living so far away I'd rarely see her. If Papa had his way, we'd never see her at all. I felt my world growing a little shaky. It was as if Vina, and others to a lesser degree, were disturbing something very special to me by uprooting themselves and going off to find their lives elsewhere.

But then I had done the same thing. Did Vina feel this way when I left Stebbinsville? Did Mama?

Of course there would be others who would leave the arena of my existence. Some day I supposed Andela and I would be far apart. Pilgrim would be just the memory of a church I once had attended. Eben and Joseph would find lives that I would never fully know about. Was it wrong of me to want to hang on to these relationships? It was like reading a great Dickens novel and wondering what happened to all the characters after the last page of the book was turned.

Yes, new characters arose to take center stage. Right now Olive Randall and Arliss Cooper were two such ones. But while I welcomed them, I still hesitated to lose others. How much more painful to lose one's friends through death. Every night I prayed for those away in the war.

Our prayers for Andela's Pavel were answered first; his regiment was mustered out in Des Moines in September. He returned home to his relieved but proud mother. His regiment had never even left the United States. Andela had been working on a painting of him in his uniform all summer which she brought to the Academy to finish. It showed the young Pavel, still babyfaced but looking strident and important. She came to my room in tears when she got the letter announcing his safe return. She was so overcome, I thought the news was of his death. When she finally spoke, she told me he was home and I cried with her.

Eben returned home in the fall also. He had spent most of his time in a camp near Chattanooga. Fever had ravaged his regiment, and took the lives of eight of his fellow soldiers. Mrs. Madison welcomed him warmly, but her mind was far away with Joseph who was on his way to Havana by Christmas.

Lottie received word from John that his regiment, which was also Don Matthews', was on its way to Manila, far away in the Phillippines. Later I heard from Don telling his version of his visit with Vina. He said she was apparently happy, but he sure couldn't understand why. She lived with three other wives in a cramped apartment and had a job in downtown San Francisco working behind the counter of a large department store. He left feeling uneasy about her, but wished her the best.

Life at Pilgrim that year faced new challenges. Reverend Kirby's son Luke had left seminary to fight in the war and now lay seriously ill in Florida. I had only once met Luke Kirby, but I felt the anguish of his father as he prayed with renewed vigor for the boys in the war. His sermons took on a more somber tone. To have dealt with the death of his wife some years ago was a blow. Those who were a part of the church then recalled how he labored in prayer when she was sick, with tears and fasting. Her death left his faith shaken. But after a while he rallied, and issued greater sermons with deeper passion than ever before. Now, however, those who knew him best feared the death of Luke would be more than the man could bear. Thus the entire church watched in prayer over the life of young Kirby as eagerly as if he had been its own son. Each Sunday I took the events at Pilgrim more seriously. Oh, I had been serious before. But the war brought us together at the church in ways we hadn't been earlier. Remembering Hilda Stone, I looked on the fraility of spirit I saw in Mrs. Madison with more compassion than previously. I had thought of her as a selfish woman who wanted to push her son ahead in the world so that he might bring her glory. But now I saw the concern she felt for him as her last living relative. I saw that if something terrible happened to him, something dreadful would also happen to her. I began to see Eben through increasingly favorable eyes. I was sorry that his lack of self-confidence was preventing some fine girl from falling in love with him. His tenderness toward Mrs. Madison was that of a son. I only wished she could see in Eben the son he wanted to be to her.

Lottie's characteristic silliness was now tempered by her concern for John. His regiment, the Fifty-first Iowa Infantry, became involved in the military occupation of Philippine villages. There was danger both to him and Don Matthews, whole letters stopped---as activity overseas curtailed his thoughts about home. The effect of the war that Fall acted like a giant hush over my world. It was like when you go into a sleeping baby's room and accidently bump against something and the baby stirs; immediately you hold your breath in stillness hoping the disturbed slumber will right itself and the baby will go back to sleep.

As Thanksgiving drew near, Andela declined my invitation to Stebbinsville. Her father was sick again---to the extent that Andela left for Thanksgiving vacation a full week early. As she left she said, "Keep us in your prayers. My family needs me during every school vacation now. But, Ann, it would give me great pleasure if you come to Spillville for Christmas. I know your own family expects you, but if there's any way..."

There was much sadness at the Wersba house with Hansel Wersba's illness and Pavel barely home, having now to assume leadership of the family and the farm.

I sincerely wished for a way I could go. I felt Andela needed me.

And as it turned out, there was a way.

In Stebbinsville for the brief Thanksgiving holiday, Martin mentioned that he wanted to go home to Philadelphia for Christmas. His brother from Ohio would be there, and his mother wanted him to come. Though neither of us spoke it, we both wished I could make the trip with him. I was anxious to meet the woman who had given Martin Pritchard to the world. That, however, would have to wait until after we were married.

As I considered Martin's trip, I remembered Andela's invitation. With Vina gone, how could I think of leaving my family? I wouldn't even have mentioned it, but on Thanksgiving Mama asked about Andela and suggested she might come to Stebbinsville for Christmas. I knew with Pavel home, Andela wouldn't consider it. So I mentioned Andela's invitation. Mama urged me to go.

"Spillville will be wonderful for you. I'm sure they have a very unique celebration," she said.

"But, Mama, I've never had a Christmas without you and Papa. And with Vina gone..." Papa's newspaper rustled at the mention of her name.

"It will do you good to have a change of scenery. We want you to go, don't we Sam?"

Papa simply said, "We'll get by."

Mama continued, "And with Martin gone this Christmas, now is the most opportune time."

Soon it was settled. When I returned to Sioux City I would tell Andela and accept her invitation.

Andela was nearly a week late in returning to the Academy. Hansel Wersba was dead.

After offering her my greatest sympathy I asked, "What will this mean for your future?"

"Father died asking me to finish school. He knows Pavel will take care of the farm. He insists I graduate."

"I'm glad," I said. "I had visions of you not returning."

"Mother resents the decision. But she cannot speak of it. She will abide by Father's wish. It is hard for me to understand the future, Ann."

"Sometimes it's *not* easy to understand. We can only trust."

At dinner that night I accepted Andela's invitation. Her countenance brightened at once.

But the overall effect of Hansel Wersba's death was to make Andela even quieter. So subdued was she in fact that even Catherine Bonacre seemed touched, and left her alone with her grief.

CHAPTER 16
CHRISTMAS 1898

As quiet as Andela usually was, our train ride across Iowa found her unusually animated. The death of her father was still very much on her heart, but her eagerness to have me share Christmas in Spillville was a definite boon to her spirits.

We talked a great deal during the trip. Singly we were normally both quiet girls, but that first night in Room K at the Academy we had established a rapport that made us as strong as sisters. She tried to prepare me for the differences I'd find in her people. She told me it would be like visiting another country---a Bohemian town on American soil. The people ate Bohemian food, danced Bohemian dances, played Bohemian card games every evening and spoke Bohemian almost exclusively.

The train took us to a small town several miles from Spillville. As we stepped down onto the small station platform we were met by a thin young man whom I recognized immediately from Andela's paintings. And though her paintings were remarkable in their lifelike renderings, I now saw that she had not done justice to her brother. Pavel was a beautiful young man with light blond hair and sad but strong blue eyes. His frame, which on others might have seemed gaunt, suited him perfectly.

I noticed that though his arms were thin, his muscles contracted tightly under his skin with the vibrancy of a young farm hand. While he was every bit the picture of a healthy young soldier, his artistry and delicate nature pierced through his eyes. His easy smile seemed to contradict all Andela had said about his melancholy nature.

Andela's eyes filled with tears as she fell into Pavel's arms. Finally as his eyes met mine he gently disengaged himself and approached with his hand extended.

"You are Ann," he said.

"I feel like I know you already, Pavel. Andela has spoken of you often," I replied. "And of course I've seen your portrait."

Pavel simply nodded as he loaded the bags into the sled and helped us up into the seat. He pulled the buffalo robes up to cover us, asking, "What is Christmas without the bitter cold, yes?"

Fresh snow lay on the ground and the sled glided over the crisp whiteness with ease, punctuated by an occasional crunch from the gathered snow. For a while Pavel and Andela spoke in Bohemian, then realizing my presence again they turned to me, Pavel asking, "You will miss your family much this Christmas?"

"Yes," I answered. "A very great deal. But it's my hope the Wersbas will be a new family to be part of. Andela is already as close to me as my sisters."

Andela brimmed with a pride I'd never seen in her before. It was as if she was showing me off to Pavel and him to me.

As the sled drove through the Main Street of Spillville, the houses and businesses in this very small town were as if from a storybook. I felt as though I was in a fairyland. As we passed one large brick building with arched windows and a huge double doorway Pavel said, "Andela has told you about when the great Dvorak came to Spillville in '93? This is the house in which he stayed. I have many fond memories here."

Andela added, "Some evenings the great composer would play his violin. Many throughout the town could hear the beautiful strains of freshly composed music from a master. Pavel would come running the mile from the farm and plant himself beneath the window listening as though he had been summoned by another world."

"We were the first to hear him compose his String Quartet. We heard selections of his great New World Symphony. It was like being part of musical history," Pavel said.

The young man proudly pointed out other landmarks as we passed them, from the noble Church of St. Wenceslas to the single shop of Benda the shoemaker. Pavel and Andela were both proud of their culture. As I was exposed to it I could appreciate the close feelings of family this community radiated. I realized that as much as Stebbinsville meant to me, so that same feeling could be multiplied several thousand times over this great American soil---wherever there was a heart that recognized a town as home. I hoped if Andela could visit Stebbinsville, she would feel the same emotion.

We pulled into the small Wersba house, as European looking as any I had seen in town.

When we entered, Andela's mother was sitting in a chair, quiet, gray, and peaceful. She smiled softly but the recent grief of her husband's death was still captured in the weary lines surrounding her pale green eyes.

Andela introduced us, her mother responding with a nod and a more personal smile.

"Happy you come to Wersba house," she said haltingly.

"As I told Pavel, I feel as if I already know you. Andela speaks of her family often," I said.

The old woman smiled again and nodded. Pavel carried my bags to the room I'd be sharing with Andela and returned with a package he put under the small bare tree waiting for decoration.

"This is something I want for you," he said, his face beaming.

"Thank you Pavel. The best present I anticipate will be to hear you play the violin," I said.

Pavel's smile relaxed and he said, "The present I have put for you under the tree will please you more, I'm certain."

Over the next several days Pavel's violin lay quiet. Andela had never known a day since he first picked it up that he hadn't played something. His reluctance worried her.

"Give him time," I suggested. "Surely he'll play for Christmas."

Our days in Spillville were swift and enjoyable. Sometimes in the evening Andela, Pavel, and I would wrap up in our warmest coats and walk into town to join in the singing of carols at small family gatherings, or watch the card games played nightly. Each evening before we left Andela suggested Pavel bring his violin, but each time he refused. When Andela asked him why he simply replied, "Not tonight."

On our excursions into town I came into even greater understanding and appreciation for the closeness of the community.

The bonds of common ancestry produced a feeling of kin amongst all, uniting them with an even greater depth than most prairie communities bound by the ties of a shared struggle. The Spillville community possessed such a bond in addition to the common past.

Yet as close as the people were, the Wersbas, not sharing the Catholic faith of their countrymen, were somewhat set apart from the rest of the community. Only a handful of the Bohemians shared their Protestant faith. Most of the people still thought of John Hus as a heretic and thus his followers were regarded as suspect.

Of course, when Hansel Wersba died all this was set aside and the men of the community turned out in a continual flow of support to the widow Wersba. Out of respect for their fellow countryman the men helped Pavel tend to the work of the Wersba farm before their own.

Pavel's return and his father's death resulted in endless days of his having to do the work of two or more men. After the first few days, Pavel encouraged the men of Spillville to return to their own farms, leaving him to carry on with the work of the small farm alone.

As Bohemians begin much of the Christmas celebration on Christmas Eve, Pavel limited his chores to the minimum on that day. The traditional Christmas Eve dish for the Wersbas was goloubtzys, which resembled a small cabbage roll cooked in tomato juice. Andela told me as she prepared them that there were seven ingredients, indeed must be seven, according to tradition. If the family was wealthy the meal could be seven separate dishes, but peasant families to which the Wersbas were more akin, ate this one delicious little roll.

As with other families in Spillville, the favorite holiday sweet was Kolace, a nut bread that filled the house with the most wonderful aroma. I memorized the way it was made, vowing to make it for Mama on my next trip home.

The entire Christmas season was even more a major celebration than I was used to. Yet for all the preparation there seemed to be a loneliness present in the Wersba house. The first Christmas after the death of a loved one is a time of renewed loss as the realization of absence is again felt. The three Wersbas were intent on *my* feelings, that I have a happy holiday with them, yet I sensed it was I who should be trying to lift their spirits.

I felt particularly bad for Pavel. His hard work drained him of each day's strength. Though he tried to be festive I knew being thrust into the headship of the household was taking its toll. It was good he could rest on Christmas Day.

After a goose dinner with all the trimmings, Bohemian style, we gathered near the small hearth to open the few presents, most of which were from Pavel who had bought them in Florida. I assumed Pavel had hastily chosen an extra something for my gift so I would be

121

remembered. But as I opened the gift and heard Pavel's story I was touched to see that he had bought it especially for me, even before we had met. Andela's love for me had prompted him to buy the gift in hopes there would someday be such an opportunity.

I opened the box and saw a shiny medallion-like pendant. It was beautiful and as I slipped it around my neck Pavel said, "Perhaps you know the story of Osceola, the great Seminole chief. He was a courageous Indian who hid his people in the swamps of Florida to avoid their being killed by white men who wished them moved to Oklahoma. This pendant was sold to me by a descendant of one of the remaining Seminoles. It is said to have belonged to Osceola. And since you're from Osceola County, I thought..."

"Pavel, this is beautiful. But it's much too nice a present. You really shouldn't have!"

"Andela has spoken of you in every letter," he said. "I feel as if you are a Wersba. And when I heard of a medallion from Osceola, I knew it must be for you."

"I'll treasure it always."

Andela said, "And now Pavel, you must give Ann the other present she wishes. You must play for her some carols."

As he reached over to stoke the fire he looked at me and said, "I would rather not. Please forgive me."

Andela glanced at her mother who sat knitting, her eyes not looking up. Pavel appeared embarrassed.

"But Pavel, you have never refused to play," Andela said.

Mrs. Wersba's knitting needles clicked stoically during the silence which followed.

Finally Andela said, "Mama, tell him to play."

The old woman remained silent, the rhythm of her knitting needles unbroken.

"Pavel, you are a musikant. You must play." Andela said.

"No, right now I must bring in more firewood," he said, rising to leave.

Andela got up to follow him but I said, "Andela, wait, let me go."

I didn't know what I'd say, but I knew Andela was too close to Pavel to speak to him without getting emotional.

I followed him out to the small shed behind the house where he was gathering an armful of wood. When he saw me he said, "It's very cold, you should go inside."

"You forget I'm an Iowa farmgirl. I know what cold is like. And I know how to carry in firewood," I said as I began to load my arms with wood.

"Perhaps so," Pavel said, "but you didn't come out here to help with the wood. You are concerned about me, is that so?"

"I'm certain you have your reasons for not playing, and I'm sure they're good ones. But Andela is your chief supporter; she deserves to know your reluctance."

"It is because of her great love for me that I cannot speak of it to her now. She cannot understand."

"She would like you to go to the conservatory in Chicago, you know."

"Yes, I know. But it is not possible."

We were silent for a minute. I held three logs in my arms. I wouldn't add more in hopes Pavel would tell me what was bothering him.

Then I said, "I didn't realize how musical you Bohemians were until Andela told me that almost everyone plays an instrument."

"Yes, that is so. Music is very important to us."

"I suspect it's even more important to you than to others in Spillville."

Pavel set his logs down. I followed his lead.

He started to look away as he spoke with a bitter edge to his voice. "Music is important in Spillville. Each one plays his instrument. During the day they farm or are merchants. At night they come home, and perhaps will take down their instruments and play for awhile. Then the instrument is replaced and not mentioned again until the next time. The next day they again go about their business and the music is forgotten. But I cannot forget. I cannot lay down my instrument to do the work of a farmer. I cannot! All the day I plow, I sow, I care for the animals, and all the day I hear the violin call me from the house. Music is as a woman a man wants to marry. And now she is like a woman spurned. If I cannot have her for a wife I will not have her as a consort. I will not have her at all."

He looked back at me as if I could provide hope. But I had none. He held out his open palms and said, "What do you see?"

I looked at the long slender fingers now sporting calluses and cuts.

"A pair of beautiful, talented hands," I answered.

"Do you, of all people, not see the hands of a farmer? Are not these the hands, perhaps of your father? Hands that will spend a lifetime sowing, harvesting, birthing calves and slaughtering them the next spring. Is this not true?"

"Yes, that's part of farming."

"And farming is my lot. My father's life was farming. And someday it will be the life of my son. It is expected of Bohemian young men to play an instrument. But to produce a Dvorak, a Kovarik, this is not for the sons of immigrant farmers."

"Who then if not you? You are the one with the talent. You are the one to be a musikant."

"Ha! All Bohemian men may be a musikant---but they still must feed their families. My mother speaks even now of the butcher's daughter, as though it was destined."

"What do you think of her and of marriage."

"I think what I am taught to think. I will marry and be a farmer."

"You speak of farming as one who dislikes it."

"No, I do not dislike it. I only relish it with the same interest others give to music. I would rather lay down my plow and pick up the violin and then return to the plow as the men in my community return to their instruments."

I sat down on the woodpile and took a breath.

"Pavel, I'm not wise when it comes to these matters. But I think we should do that which pleases us while young. We won't always have our youth. It fades quickly, so say those who have been where we are today. Some in my family, even my own father, doubted the wisdom of my education. There is a man who wanted to marry me. Some thought I should forget four years of school---they even vowed they'd be wasted years. Then when I got to the Academy there were those, students and teachers, who would have had me forget my writing aspirations. But I have a passion for writing, there is a promise of happiness for me as I write. I can feel it inside. Surely that is the way you feel about your music?"

"Yes, yes of course, but..."

"Then you must trust that our God will provide for us as we act on the right impulses He gives us. He would no more give you the talent for music and have you remain a farmer than he would give a violin to a farm man and ask him to make a living of it."

"But when mothers are expecting..."

"You love your mother?"

"Of course."

"If she knew your pain, would it please her? I'm not suggesting that you abandon farming or music. But you must do that which satisfies the hunger God has placed in you."

For a minute neither of us spoke. It was quiet outside. High above us stars shone as though they were eavesdropping witnesses. From inside the house we could barely hear the rapid Bohemian speech of mother and daughter---it was like a comforting echo. I listened to them as I watched Pavel gather his wood again. In the voices we heard, lay a part of him. The choices he made would effect those dear women whom he, and now I, both loved. I didn't envy men such choices. I thought about Martin. Men his age were fighting a war. Some of his childhood friends had gone to Harvard and Yale and were wealthy now. Some of his seminary colleagues were pastoring large prestigious churches.

Martin would never be rich. He would probably never pastor any large city church. His choices had not been popular with some. Yet God's blessing was on Martin and he knew it. And that was enough. He had a congregation who loved him, and I loved him.

I determined never to exact from my children such destinies as I would choose. Matters of such import are best left to the workings of God in the heart of each man and woman.

Pavel and I went in the house with our arms loaded with wood. I saw him eye the violin case by the parlor door as he passed by.

Andela and I left two days later, still never hearing Pavel play.

On our return to the Academy I had several letters from home awaiting me---and a card from Vina and Charles. Vina had taken yet another job, three in such a short time! And this one was the best yet, working in a dress factory. She told me she planned to repay Mama's hundred dollars before Papa found out about it. Vina sounded so happy, just as Elsie had when she first left home.

New Year's Eve came on a Saturday that year and Pilgrim was having a watchnight service to usher in the new year. Just as Andela and I were about to leave the Academy for church, Lottie came up to us in the lobby and said, "Before you go, you should know the news."

She lowered her head and as she started to speak I felt surely Luke Kirby had passed on, but I was dazed to hear her say, "Joseph Madison has died in the war."

Andela and I couldn't speak for several seconds. Lottie said, "Mrs. Madison will not likely be there tonight, but I'm sure she'll be remembered as the prayer service begins. She is not taking the news well."

"And Eben?" Andela asked. "How is he taking it?"

"Very hard also. It's as if he lost a brother. He wishes

it had been him."

"How did he die?" I asked.

"Like most of the rest, of the fever," Lottie said.

We rode slowly to the church, each thinking through the terrible implications for Mrs. Madison, her last living relative tragically taken from her.

Andela said, "Sometimes, I just don't understand the ways of God. Really, I don't."

"Sometimes the reasons can't be known--not ever, in this life," I said.

"For the past several days I have been so grateful for Pavel's return and yet concerned for his violin, I had forgotten that feeling of dread I used to think about while Pavel was gone. Sometimes at night I'd dream he died. I would wake up sweating, with that awful feeling and a vision of his lifeless body on a faraway field of battle. I thought I'd never forget that feeling, Ann. Now Mrs. Madison has that feeling, yet it is not a dream. And there is nothing we can do."

"Perhaps in time," I suggested.

"I think for Mrs. Madison," Andela said, "time will not be a friend. If anything it may only become worse. I fear she will dwell on it and it will become a continual thorn in her heart."

The church was full and, though in churches across America there were similar congregations exuding the joy of the approaching year, there was a pall over Pilgrim Presbyterian that night.

CHAPTER 17
SPRING 1899

More and more I found the name of Arliss Cooper in the pages of my journal. His influence on my writing was immeasurable. And although he was a fine teacher, it was more his encouragement that steadied my writing. I wrote assigned stories knowing that a teacher who really cared would be reading them. Mr. Cooper also gave me a sense of audience. He advised me to picture my readers, usually young women, and try to see my story through their eyes. Mrs. Whitely continued to be a support but I soon understood why the stories she had written had failed. She never had received nor learned to appreciate the tenets of good journalistic writing that Arliss Cooper was teaching me.

I was also learning about the great force of tragedy in a person's life. At the time I supposed it was as an aid to my writing, not realizing the sadness that would come to my own life only a year later. Instead, week after week I watched the drama of Mrs. Madison as she tried to come to terms with the loss of her last son. Reverend Kirby counseled her as best he could. His son Luke had survived the war after all, but came home weak and minus his left leg. His once pert and happy countenance was now broken. It seemed when his leg was taken, a part of his spirit went with it. He refused to return to the seminary, but rather sat at home much of the time doing little.

Yet he was alive. Joseph Madison was not. And any

comfort Reverend Kirby offered Henrietta fell on deaf ears. She would have gladly accepted Joseph home, minus *any* limbs, just to have him with her again.

Eben was also at a loss concerning Mrs. Madison. As he had earlier lost his family, he now counted Mrs. Madison as a mother. I knew she appreciated Eben's concern, but in her grief she could hardly help closing him off.

Sitting in church with Andela one Sunday morning I looked over to see tears in her eyes.

"What's wrong?" I whispered.

She looked to her right toward where Eben sat with Mrs. Madison, his head bowed, lost in thought, oblivious to Reverend Kirby's sermon.

"Eben. I worry for him," she said.

After the service we both approached Eben. I tried to be cheerful. Andela in her sympathy was as melacholy as he was.

On the spur of the moment I found myself asking, "Eben, Andela and I would like to come home with you and Mrs. Madison for a Sunday dinner. May we? We'll do all the cooking, we just need the kitchen."

Without feeling Eben said, "It's fine with me, but you best ask Mrs. Madison. She don't seem to welcome much company these days."

I left Andela with Eben and found Mrs. Madison with Reverend Kirby. When their conversation ended I took advantage of the minister's presence and said, "Reverend Kirby, I was just suggesting to Eben that Andela and I invite ourselves over to cook a superb dinner for him and Mrs. Madison. Don't you concur that a good hearty meal would round out a nearly perfect Lord's Day?"

Reverend Kirby was no doubt surprised by my boldness. I was known in the church for my reticience, not my brashness. After a moment's silence he said, "Well yes, certainly. In fact, if we're inviting ourselves to dine at Mrs. Madison's perhaps I should invite myself and

Luke. It's been a good while since we had two such fine young ladies prepare our meal."

By inviting himself Reverend Kirby prevented Mrs. Madison's refusal. But I had been hoping for just the four of us. To have Luke along might remind Mrs. Madison of her own loss. But the arrangements were made.

Andela and I rode with Reverend Kirby and Luke, who seemed reluctant to go. And as the day wore on Luke continued to seem ill at ease for some reason. He and Eben had never really been friends. Luke was normally quite outgoing, but with Eben's quietness, even the most gregarious man might find difficulty making friends. Yet a friend was just what Eben needed most.

Still the afternoon was a success in that it forced Mrs. Madison and Eben to be more sociable than they would have been otherwise. Perhaps with such continued prodding Mrs. Madison would begin to count her blessings, starting with Eben.

At the Academy my attention was turned again toward Catherine Bonacre. With each passing term she seemed to settle into a worse mood. Andela was always there with an excuse for her behavior. As her roommate this term, she tried to be an encouragement, but Catherine continually shut her out. Again she began making rude remarks about Andela's heritage. I asked myself over and over what lesson was there for me in the life of Catherine? How would Martin deal with her if she were one of his congregation?

Finally in April events began to occur that would end Catherine's days at the Academy. One Friday night she broke the Academy curfew for the third night in a row. Early Saturday morning she was summoned to Miss Button's office. Catherine insisted she was an adult and would stay out as long as she pleased. Such boldness left Miss Button no alternative but to ask her not to return in the Fall, a generous offer, since many of the students felt Catherine should be asked to leave immediately. Miss Button was defying Dr. Sinclair's wishes, but to allow continued disobedience demoralized everyone else. Miss Button believed in the utmost offering of grace with the expectation that the result in a repentant heart would be restoration. Catherine, however, was not repentant. The day finally came in May, only three weeks before the end of term, when another confrontation and another summons to Miss Button's office resulted in Catherine angrily packing her bags. The cause of this rift was her open rudeness and name-calling to Artemis and Milly, each of whom had held their own tongues many times during the treatment they received at her hand.

Catherine had found a young man, apparently, and it was to him she would go. Her uncle wanted nothing to do with her and handed over to her the remainder of her inheritance, which had been entrusted to his keeping until such time as he deemed appropriate to give it to her. With her leaving school he simply determined to wash his hands of his niece and gave her a rumored amount of nearly five thousand dollars.

The young man who had taken up with Catherine was a dockhand known only as "Buck." According to Eben, most of the dockworkers had little to do with him. He was a large bulky man, given to much profanity and drinking. We all remarked that it would be a very strong man, or a weak one, who would take up with Catherine.

The night she left, Andela begged Catherine to reconsider, to apply herself more diligently to her studies. To move out with this Buck was a grave mistake, Andela said. When that advice went unheeded, Andela urged Catherine to at least leave her money on deposit in the bank and not to let Buck use any of it.

But Catherine had found a man who would give her attention. That was all that mattered. Nothing anyone said could dissuade her.

At breakfast the morning after Catherine's departure both Miss Button and Andela had red eyes. Both hoped that perhaps after a while Catherine would see her folly and ask to be given another chance in the Fall.

131

For days afterwards a strange quiet fell upon the Academy. For so long we had endured Catherine, even grown accustomed to her loud complaints. Now with her gone we suffered mixed feelings---relief, yes, but concern for her too.

By graduation that spring, all of us, including Miss Button and Andela, had come to accept that Catherine's mistake was going to turn out more serious than we thought. It was rumored she was pregnant. She would not return to the Academy in the Fall, or ever. Miss Button had known of a great many young women who quit the Academy, even some who were asked to leave. But this case troubled her deeply.

As we gathered for another graduation ceremony, we third year students were especially aware that only too soon our turn would come. Miss Button, as always, rejoiced with those who graduated but mourned the loss of young women she had come to love over the past four years. I too would miss them. Each young woman brought a new awareness to me of the wonder of God's creativity in shaping a human being. Like divine snowflakes, no two young women were alike.

As Dr. Sinclair handed each young woman her diploma I daydreamed about their futures. Would they find happiness? Had the years at the Academy prepared them for what lay ahead? Would their lives be marked with sorrow or would blessings follow this one or that one?

As Miss Button rose to greet each of the girls, hankie in hand, Lottie leaned over to me and said, "Gosh, you'd think after all these years she'd be used to it."

I smiled and nodded, but I understood Miss Button perfectly.

We adjourned to the Parlor for refreshments. I went up to the graduates and wished them well, giving each a hug, realizing that as many of them returned to their faraway homes and began the next part of their lives, I'd never ever see most of them again. Frances Means was going to marry a young accountant from her hometown and move to New York. Polly Prentiss was taking a job in Washington D.C., Emily Richfield would continue her schooling at an eastern University. I could almost feel the pride of accomplishment in the breast of each.

Andela and I decided to stay on through the Sunday after graduation to attend one more service at Pilgrim. Reverend Kirby asked us to, and we agreed.

The sermon was on forgiveness and I supposed there must have been a reason why Andela and I were meant to hear the message but I really couldn't think of anyone I needed to forgive. Reverend Kirby said we needed to forgive as often as we wanted God to forgive us. My thoughts turned to Papa and Vina. Mama had just written that Vina was expecting a baby early next year.

Charles had been home from the war since January. He was working steadily as a dockhand on the San Francisco waterfront---and Vina, my little kid sister, was going to have a baby.

I had received a letter from Mama from which I could tell how much she longed to be with Vina when the baby was born, but Papa would never allow it. Mama would have to defy him to see her own grandchild. How Papa could be so unforgiving stumped me. And then I realized it also meant Papa wasn't allowing God to forgive him.

As the sermon ended I found out the real reason Andela and I were asked to stay, as Reverend Kirby asked Lottie and John Hammond to come to the front of the church. When they did so, he asked them to face the congregation as he announced their engagement.

Afterward Andela and I scolded Lottie for keeping it such a good secret from all of us at the Academy. She gave me a hug and said, "It was hardest to keep it from you two.

"You will be my attendants, won't you?"

"Of course," we said.

"When is the day?" Andela asked.

"You know me! Always looking for excitment. I want

133

to be married New Year's Eve---Just think, not only will John and I start out a new year as man and wife, but a whole new century! You can come back from Christmas vacation in time, can't you?"

"We wouldn't miss it," Andela said.

"Leave it to Lottie!" I said as I gave her a hug.

Eben had been standing off to one side as Lottie told us her plans. When she finished he took me aside and said, "Ann, I want to wish you a happy summer. We miss you here when you're gone." His face was beginning to redden as I said, "I miss being here. But I love my Stebbinsville home too. It's hard to have your heart in two places at once."

"I know what you mean," he said softly.

"How?" I asked.

"Joseph was like a brother to me. Mrs. Madison is like a mother. I can bring her no happiness, but I will watch over her for the rest of her life. I owe her that. Yet I long to farm again. I don't like living in the city. If I could save my wages for a while I could buy a farm."

"There are always one or two spreads for sale up Stebbinsville way. I could ask around this summer," I suggested.

"I could never get Mrs. Madison back on a farm. And my place is with her. With Joseph gone she has no one but me---and yet I'm not really important to her."

"No, I suppose no one can replace Joseph." I wished there was something I could say, but it was true that Mrs. Madison didn't appreciate Eben. Just a month earlier I listened as she responded to a new church member who had asked about her son, Eben.

"Oh, Eben isn't my son," she said. "I have no sons. Eben is just the son of neighbor I used to have. Now he is my helper." She made it sound as though Eben was merely a hired hand. Yet I knew he took no money from Mrs. Madison but rather freely gave of his pay to help support her.

"I suppose there was a message for you in the sermon this morning," I said.

"Forgiveness is always a good word, though I bear no hard feelings for Mrs. Madison. It is just as you said, it's hard to have your heart in two places."

"Eben, I suspect God will work it out for you some way. It can't be right for you to be such a good farmer and have to live in the city." Eben showed no emotion. He smiled and said, "Again, may this be a fine summer for you." Then he turned away to find Mrs. Madison and take her home.

I told Andela of Eben's concern on our way back to the Academy. She said nothing, but I knew her sensitive nature was as worried for Eben as for her former roommate.

That afternoon Andela took me to her room.

"I have something to show you," she said as she pulled a large frame from her closet.

As she turned the canvas toward me I was able to see again the unique talent Andela had for imputing a breath of life into the midst of a picture frame.

It was of Catherine---and magnificent, though not yet completed.

"I began it the day she left. Do you think she will like it?" Andela asked.

"Oh yes. Of course she will. And you did it from memory? Without her posing?"

Andela nodded. "I do my best work when the subject poses. But, of course, that was not possible. I will finish it this summer. In the fall, you will come with me to deliver it to her?"

"Yes. I can barely wait to see her face. Surely this will soften her."

"Yes, that's my hope---I want Catherine to know I love her."

"She's just so hard to love. I admire your patience with her."

We resolved to visit Catherine the first week of September, even before classes started. And best of all, Andela would be my roommate in the Fall, again.

We both took early morning trains on Monday. Martin

met my train, took me home, and stayed for supper. It took less time to catch up on town news this time. So many of the events were happening to people I didn't know.

The news that mattered the most was that Ethan and Hilda had sold their place and moved into town. There was just too much to remind them of the children out on the farm. Ethan was working part time at the livery stable and Hilda helped out a bit at the hardware, though there was talk of her opening a bakery. Her German delicacies had a reputation throughout Osceola County. She had aged since I had seen her last summer, rarely laughed or teased as she once did. She was a different woman. Mama and I mourned for her yet.
Mama and I mourned for her yet.

The other big news was Elsie's third pregnancy which paralleled Vina's---both babies being due early the next year. The former we could readily discuss anytime, the latter only when Papa was out of the room.

Don Matthews and Lloyd Thurston, whom I didn't know, had returned to Stebbinsville as war heroes. Don re-opened his fix-it shop and was prospering, as well as seeing Florence McCasland regularly.

The farmers had also prospered greatly these last few seasons. And as they prospered, so did Bullard Hardware and Feed. I worked steadily all summer, trying to convince Papa that my life in the city hadn't turned me into a woman of ease.

CHAPTER 18
FALL 1899

Come September, a surprise awaited me at the Academy, in the installation of what Papa considered another "fool contraption." A telephone box had been connected in the hallway. I had never used one before and it was made clear this one was to be used for emergencies only. That, of course, went without saying. Barely one of us knew anyone who had a telephone. So who would we call anyway?

In Stebbinsville there were two or three around town ---one at the City Hall and one at the new hospital. Mama was toying with the notion of having one put in the Hardware as an attraction, but Papa wouldn't hear of it.

The new telephone at the Academy was on the wall a full week before any of us heard it ring. And that call was for Miss Button from Dr. Sinclair. Still, it was quite a novelty, and intrigued us as it perched clumsily on the wall.

I was one of the first women back to the Academy in September. As such, and because I was a Senior, I assumed the role of greeter of the new girls. It was the very position Rowena Gainesborough held three years earlier.

I smiled inwardly at how shy and nervous the new girls were. It seemed only yesterday I stood in the same entryway with my simple straw braid hat, just as nervous as these new arrivals. Remembering the coolness I felt from Rowena, I went out of my way to make them feel genuinely at ease. I tried to memorize each girl's name and hometown as she spoke it.

As the first few days went by and I got to know the girls, I was able to pick the ones I thought would succeed. I could tell which were merely husband hunting, which were serious students. I even fancied I could tell which would soon be members of Pilgrim.

Miss Button, of course, was an expert in discerning the young women when they enrolled. As I worked in her office I gained an even greater appreciation for her subtle sense of humor, and her sense of motherhood toward these young women she considered her "girls."

I again saw just how close she felt to every girl when she said how disappointed she was that Catherine Bonacre hadn't been heard from. Miss Button was like the prodigal's father, standing at the gate watching, waiting.

When Andela arrived three days after I did, she showed me her completed portrait of Catherine. My impression was that Andela saw each person she painted in their best possible manner as though they were perfect human beings. Perhaps this made her less than a realistic painter, I don't know. But when I saw the expression she gave Catherine, I knew she had done right.

To Andela, as seen in the painting, Catherine carried no hard shell. Andela gave us a Catherine with a pure heart---which is how Andela saw her.

That was the undefinable quality of her paintings---to see through exterior facades to the inner person---as perhaps God saw.

Thinking about it, my hope became that, as Catherine saw the portrait each day, she too would be able to see herself as she was meant to be. How could this not effect her for the good?

The next morning we left the Academy for Catherine's. My duties as greeter were over and the only appointment of the day was to attend the school-wide orientation at two in the afternoon.

The address we had for Catherine was down near the docks; in fact, in the very part of town I had just explained to the Freshmen women that they were not to be seen. Miss Button, of course, gave Andela and I dispensation for this trip, in addition to a note of concern she'd written to Catherine.

After we got off the streetcar we had to walk several blocks down fearful streets of shabby tenements. Our consolation was the thought that the element we most feared were mostly nocturnal and were at the moment probably sleeping.

It hadn't occurred to us that Catherine might be sleeping; it was nearly eleven when we arrived at the four story brown building. It took several seconds after our knock for Catherine to answer.

Andela and I were both shaken by her appearance. She stood before us in no more than bedclothes, her yellow hair strewn and matted, her eyes heavy, the life seeping from them. She was indeed expectant, confirming rumors.

She so contradicted the portrait Andela was bringing that I wondered if we should give it to her. It might only hurt her more.

"Well," she asked, "What do you two want?"

"To see you, of course." Andela said as though we'd seen her only yesterday. "May we come in? Just for a moment?" And then without waiting for an answer, my shy Andela simply walked in. I followed, a little doubtful of our mission.

The small apartment was unkempt. There was very little furniture.

"How have you been getting on?" Andela asked.

"How does it look like I've been getting on? Actually I'm doing well. I really do well."

"This is from Miss Button," I said, handing her the note.

"Ha! Miss Button," Catherine said, tearing the note without reading it.

"She cares about you," I said.

"We all do," Andela added

"Care? Care? I don't think any of you care for a lick, b'sides your own selves. And who's to blame? That's the way, isn't it? Care for yourself, no one else."

Catherine sat down on a small tattered divan.

"Who's that?" a male voice called from the next room.

"Go back to sleep. Two students from the Academy, they're selling raffle tickets. Isn't that right, girls?"

"So this is the life you've chosen?" Andela asked boldly.

"Buck and I are a pair. We do the lookin' out for each other---that's all we need. We don't need no one else."

Andela pulled the framed picture from the brown paper covering it.

"I have something for you," Andela said.

Catherine looked puzzled and said, "What would you have that I want?"

Andela faced the portrait toward Catherine.

Catherine's eyes widened for a second, and she started to speak. She rose from her seat, walked over to Andela and picked up the picture. After a minute of quiet she handed the portrait back to Andela.

"So you think that is me?"

"Do you?" Andela asked.

"No, no I don't. I don't know who I am," her voice rising as in anger. "This is not Catherine Bonacre in this painting. Andela, you're a fool! You've wasted a great many hours."

"I think I have not," said Andela.

From the other room the male voice called, "What's going on out there?"

"Nothing," Catherine answered, "They're just leaving." She walked to the door and opened it.

"Please don't come back," she said.

Andela set the picture against the wall as we started to leave.

"I don't want it!" Catherine said.

Andela, near tears, looked at her and said, "Then you may discard it."

The door was shut firmly behind us. The trip back to the Academy was long and silent. Miss Button heard our account and just turned away to other duties without a word.

Classes began on a Wednesday due to the delay of one of the eastbound trains. For this, my final year, I had chosen another course in American History, a class in debating, a required class in Elementary Science I had been putting off, Miss Button's Deportment, and a continuation of my writing studies with Mr. Cooper, under whose constant prodding and encouragement I was beginning to feel more confident as a writer. There were fourteen of us who now met for an early class on "The Way of the Writer." I suspected the popularity of a class that had little interest only a year earlier was due in large part to Mr. Cooper's striking good looks and genial nature. His name was on the lips of many a young woman gathered round the supper tables.

I was surprised that Lottie was content with John now that someone the caliber of Arliss Cooper was around. If he had been teaching during our first year, it's possible that Lottie and John would not have become engaged. Yet now Lottie hung on John's arm steadily. As to Mr. Cooper's romantic notions, he expressed interest in none of our young women, much to the regret of many.

By October Mr. Cooper had encouraged me to send out several of my stories to magazines, all of which were promptly returned with a publisher's sharp note of rejection. I then put them right back in the mail to other magazines---yet they would again return to me like perfect boomerangs. Had it not been for Mr. Cooper's unwavering support I'm sure I'd have given up after the first rejection. As it was, I began to dread each day's mail. When I discovered a rejection slip, or worse, two, I was always depressed until class Friday morning when I would again receive a dose of his encouragement to persevere ahead.

One day in early December, one I shall never forget, I left my last class of the day, Deportment, downcast. We had spent the entire session on wedding etiquette and customs. It all seemed so futile. I just wanted a simple wedding in a simple church. Yet I had to sit through an hour discussion on color matching, flower selection, invitation wording and such.

After class I walked absently downstairs and took up my mail without regard. A note from Vina, one rejection and one rather nondescript envelope addressed to me but with no return address.

I opened the note from Vina first. She was fine. There was a lot of rain these days, she said. Her pregnancy was advancing on schedule, she'd heard from Mama that my writing interest was at an all-time high and she wished me all the luck in the world.

I moved on to the rejection---it was very much like the other twenty-two I had in my dresser drawer. Last I turned to the unfamiliar envelope. It looked so unimportant and, of course, I had become so accustomed to the rejections that it never occurred to me that one day I might actually receive a letter accepting one of my stories. Yet here it was---the *Youth Companion* liked my story of "Love Comes to Marjorie" and was sending me five dollars. It would appear in the Spring issue and I would be sent two copies along with the five dollars.

I must have stood in the parlor with the letter in my hand for several minutes in disbelief. Perhaps it was a mistake, I told myself. They must have mixed up my story with someone else's, but no, the title was right--it must be my story! Surely it can't be! To be paid money for a story from my own head. How could it be?

I raced upstairs to tell Andela.

"It's happened!" I yelled. "Oh Andela, it's happened. I've sold a story. I've actually sold a story!" I grabbed her and picked her up, spinning her around before setting her down. I'm sure neither she nor anyone else had seen me so animated. Before Andela could speak I ran out the door and down the hall knocking on doors and

142

laughing. I was acting like I'd forgotten every lesson in deportment Miss Button had ever given. I ran back down the stairs and found several young women gathered at the foot of the stairs with Miss Button in front of them. They all had a quizzical expression on their face, all except for Miss Button who must have guessed my cause for joy. As I got to the foot of the stairs she grabbed me eagerly and with almost as much excitement as I had, she gave me a long happy hug.

"We knew you'd do it dear. We never doubted," she said. I stood back and looked in her face and realized that it was true. She never doubted I'd succeed. For any of us who had a dream, she was more than eager to believe in that dream with us.

Andela stood beside me, now smiling. She understood like some of the others couldn't. It was like she had sold a prized painting. It was someone who's opinion mattered saying your time had been well spent.

"Oh, I can't wait to tell Mr. Cooper!" I said. "Just wait till he hears the news. And I owe this to his class---and to you Miss Button, I'm so glad you took a chance and offered this class."

"You're welcome my dear. But the one you really need to thank is Mrs. Whitely. She's the one who did the convincing."

"Oh, Mrs. Whitely, of course. Wait until she hears! Oh I have so many people to thank. And wait til Papa hears, and Mama---and of course Martin! He'll be so proud!"

The young women each offered me hearty congratulations and, the excitement waning, Andela and I started back up the stairs. I was mischievously thinking to myself about the others I would like to hear this news--- for instance, Elsie---what would she say now? Would this vindicate education in her eyes? How about Papa? And Mr. Hoffman? I was ashamed of myself for the way I wanted to take him my acceptance letter and say, "I *can* write! I *can* write!"

But I realized it was a more pleasant thought to share

this kind of happiness with those who could appreciate it best. James and Julia Evans came to mind. Two copies would simply not be enough. I wanted to rush right out to the man who sold the *Youth Companion* over on Douglas Street and tell him to save every copy of the Spring issue for me. I'd spend every cent of the five dollars on copies of the *Youth Companion.*

I barely slept that night. I decided not to write home about my sale---Christmas was soon coming and I'd be home in a couple of weeks and could tell them all in person. But as I thought about tomorrow when I could tell Mr. Cooper and Miss Whitely (and even Mr. Hoffman), I found sleep eluded me. By the time I was in bed I had read the letter so many times I had it memorized, so I lay there mentally reading it over and over to myself till sleep finally did come.

The next morning I ate breakfast at Olive Randall's table. She looked up at me as I sat down and said coolly, "The world famous writer arrives for breakfast."

My success certainly didn't impress Olive. She had started in the writing class as one of those with none too subtle designs on Mr. Cooper---designs which she ascribed to all the rest of us. That my interest in writing proved genuine was to her a mark of defeat. There were so many who praised my efforts and supported me, I suppose such an attitude shouldn't have bothered me. But I had been brought up to believe that if you went about doing good in this world and behaved yourself, that people would respect your successes. I was finding that not true---Catherine Bonacre, even Rowena Gainesborough, and now Olive Randall were showing me a side of human nature I thought only occured in Mr. Dickens' novels. Papa had a contrary nature but he wasn't like Olive, deliberately rude to people in their successes.

After breakfast I hurried up to Mrs. Whitely's classroom.

She was sitting at her desk going over papers. Her fingers curled up under her chin motionless.

"Knock knock. May I see you for a minute?" I said as I entered.

"Of course Ann." She looked up from her papers with a sigh. "These new young women get more careless every year. What will I do with them?"

"I suppose you'll teach them better, just as you have me."

"And what may I ask does that vague smile mean? You're up to something, I can tell," she said.

I tried to look as serious as I could as I held up the letter of acceptance. "This, Mrs. Whitely, is your doing. You're the one to answer for this."

Unmoved, Mrs. Whitely said, "I am, am I? And just what have we here?" she asked as she reached up and took the letter from my hand.

As she read it her characteristic fingers were soon in motion under chin. When she finished she reached into her drawer and pulled out a hankie and dabbed her eyes.

"Ann, I'm so proud, I don't know what to say. Except that I knew you could do this---and much more. By my word, someday you'll be showing me a book instead of a letter."

"When and if that day comes, I'll be giving you a copy, that'll be for certain. But let's not go boasting about the future. If I never sell another thing, at least I've done this. It is almost enough."

Young women were starting to come into the room for class, so I gave Mrs. Whitely a kiss and went on to my first class---writing. Mr. Cooper stood at the blackboard. I was a little more embarrassed to show him the letter than I had been Mrs. Whitely. He read it and broke into a wide grin.

"Ann, this is wonderful. Just wonderful!" He beamed with pride for me. I hoped I could count on similar looks from Papa and Martin.

As soon as the class was in order Mr. Cooper held up my letter and made some lofty statements about talent and perseverance, all the while congratulating me on my sale.

After class when I came up to get the letter he said, "Ann, this really does call for a celebration. May I call on you this Saturday for dinner?"

My face reddened. Mr. Cooper was my teacher. I was sure there must be some rule against socializing with students, but Mr. Cooper wasn't regular faculty and I doubted whether he would have held such a rule in regard anyway.

"I understand you're engaged to a young man back home. But surely he wouldn't mind a congratulatory dinner under such circumstances," he said.

"I...I suppose not. But I really don't think we should."

"Oh, propriety, I suppose," he said cynically. "Well then, how about dessert?"

I didn't want to disappoint him. It was his reward too. But I couldn't go by myself with him, it just wouldn't seem right. My silence urged him to say, "Well then how about if I take you and a friend of your choosing. That should stop the tongues, shouldn't it?"

So it was agreed that Andela, Lottie and I would be taken out to dinner, and returned no later than eight o'clock on Saturday.

Lottie looked forward to it with glee. There was still enough of the adventuresome single girl in her to want to be seen in public with a man like Mr. Cooper. Andela was more a proper chaperone. She knew and accepted my reservations about going out with Mr. Cooper. I think she and I both breathed easier when we finally returned home on Saturday night.

As we came into the entryway Mr. Cooper asked if he might have a word with me in the parlor. Andela and Lottie went up to their rooms, Lottie giving me a clever wink on her way up. I hoped this conversation would be brief. I couldn't bear it if I should become the subject of rumors.

As we entered the parlor three or four first-year students sitting at one of the study tables looked up at us and back down at their books with a smile that made me uncomfortable.

146

As we sat down on the cushioned bench near the hearth Mr. Cooper said, "Ann I wanted to tell you how much I appreciate teaching you. I doubt if I'd have returned this year had I not been certain you'd be here. You're a fine writer. And if you continue, someday you'll be a great writer."

"You flatter me," I said. "But I'll never be a great anything. I'll be content to live a full happy life. Many people don't even enjoy that privilege."

"Wouldn't success as a writer help make that life happier?"

"Perhaps. I'm sure it would make me feel I'd reached a great personal goal. I'd feel I'd done something I was meant to do. But Martin and I believe true happiness comes from other sources than occupational success. Look at Mr. Poe for example, a successful writer, but a very unhappy human being."

"Ah yes, you find your brand of happiness in the church."

"Not the church. But what it represents."

"And that would be?"

"Spiritual truths, I suppose, would be one way of saying it."

A characteristic cynical smile lit his face. "The unseen things. I do have trouble with such concepts. To me this life, this earthly life, is grand enough. I plan to get out of it all it can offer."

I understood what he meant, but answered, "I plan the same. I too love life. But to love the gift of life without a care to loving the Giver seems pointless. How much greater the enjoyment of life when lived out from its true source."

"The words of a talented writer if ever I heard them," he said with a short laugh. "You'll be a great fiction writer for sure."

"I'm sorry you feel that way. I'm not talking about fiction." I began to be a little irritated. He made me feel like a child. "It's getting rather late, perhaps we should say goodnight."

"Oh, I've angered you. The last thing I meant to do. You see, Ann, I want a chance to win you over. I'd like to call on you again, if I may."

"Mr. Cooper, I'm engaged," I said, feeling the red return to my face.

"Ah, but women are notorious for changing their minds."

I rose and said, "Good evening, Mr. Cooper. I enjoyed our celebration very much."

"But not enough to consider dining with me alone?"

"I'm afraid not."

Mr. Cooper rose and we walked toward the door. Then, suddenly before I knew it, he turned and kissed me firmly on the cheek, winked slyly and said, "You really must call me Arliss. All my close acquaintances do." Then he left.

I stood frozen to the spot, both flattered and furious.

CHAPTER 19
WINTER 1899

As deeply as my letter of acceptance moved me, a week later, just before I was to go home for Christmas, I received another letter, the news of which would eventually have an equally resounding effect on my life.

I sat quietly on my bed as I read from Mama:

It appears that I am once again to bear a child for your father. Of course such news is a great joy. Yet I know only too well that I am a grandmother, and past the age when I thought I would be anticipating labor once again. This baby, now forming, drains me of my daily energies. Such is not news, all my babies were exacting on my body. But this one ....

Dr. Matthews insisted Mama rest most of her time, the letter went on to say. Household duties were given over to Grandma who had temporarily moved in to direct Lucy and Mae. Poor Grandma. She was gone from her own home more often than not. Papa, according to a letter from Grandma, was silent about the pregnancy.

I left for Christmas in Stebbinsville with greater eagerness than ever before. Not only to be a help to Mama but also I needed to be away from the Academy. The news of Mr. Cooper's attentions toward me spread rapidly through the Academy. Lottie was a source of gossip. When I confronted her about it, she simply said,

"Oh, Ann it's nothing. We all know you love Martin, but what's a girls' school without a rich piece of news like this?" She meant it in innocence, but I couldn't help but feel the import of her words as though there were real cause for alarm. I felt like my writing class was ruined. I couldn't look at Mr. Cooper without feeling his kiss anew. Miss Button heard of the incident and threatened to dismiss Mr. Cooper. But I couldn't have that happen. He was an excellent instructor, and the only one in all of Sioux City who could do as much good for aspiring writers. It was important that he stay.

The day before I left, he asked me to remain after class. As I approached his desk he said, "I understand I've caused you some embarrassment. I'm sorry for that, really sorry."

"It's not your fault, I guess. Girls will talk."

"Ann, I'm not very good at speaking. I can write well, but I guess I only know how to say the wrong thing. I meant everything I said to you that night in the parlor, I really do care for you. More than any other woman I've known. I was, am, grasping at chances to see if I can find a place in your heart. As for your Martin, I understand why he loves you. You're quite a wonderful person. But, dash it all, Ann, surely you can see that you and I, with our interest in writing, could make a great team, a great couple. I just would like a chance to win you over."

I didn't know what to say. When, as a girl on the farm, I first knew that I wanted to be a writer, I longed for someone like Mr. Cooper who could share my passion for books and writing. At first I thought it might be Mr. Evans, but when that proved not to be the case, and I became aware of my love for Martin, I gave up on finding a person to share my dreams with, other than someone such as Mrs. Whitely.

"Will you give me a chance?" Mr. Cooper asked.

Just then Miss Button came in and said, "Ann, haven't you another class to attend?"

Without speaking I turned and went to my speech

class. Miss Button stayed to have a talk with Mr. Cooper, presumably about his friendliness with me.

It was with great relief that I stepped off the train in Stebbinsville for the Christmas season. The work of the next several days in helping Mama ready for the holiday, plus the acclaim for my story being sold, proved to be just the tonic I needed.

Mama, however, noticed I wasn't totally at ease. One morning she called me to her bedside and drew out of me the whole story of Arliss and his intentions.

"And how do you genuinely feel about him, Ann? Is he a nice young man?"

"Oh yes, very nice. I think the world of Arliss Cooper. And he's so right when he says we've got a lot in common. Mama, to find someone who can believe in me as a writer, it's like a dream come true."

Mama took my hand. "I know dear, but do you love him?"

"No....That is, I don't think so. I don't know. I should say no. As alike as we are in our writing, we're also very different in some of the other important areas. He's not a believing man. He thinks church is a waste of time. How can I even be thinking of loving him? No, I don't love him. But oh, Mama, he makes me dream big about the future, as if by loving him I could really be a great writer. Why, if it wasn't for Arliss, I mean Mr. Cooper, I would never have sold that story. It was he who kept after me, kept believing in me."

I was silent for a minute, then continued, "Mama do you remember what it was like when we first came to Iowa, how you and Papa were at odds?"

Mama nodded.

"What would you have given right then if Papa was the kind of man who really understood you and wanted to help you be someone, someone other than just his maid and cook?"

Mama sat up in bed. "Listen Ann, I know how things must have looked to you all these years. You think my

151

life has been hard, and perhaps so. But I was never just a maid and a cook. I loved and still do love Sam Bullard. And though I disagree with him sometimes, I love him just the way he is, burr under his saddle and all. Now, there's not many women who can say that they've found a man they can love and be happy with like that. I don't regret a single day of being married to your father. I once heard it said, 'the good is the enemy of the best.' I believe that. I could have married someone else, two times over. But I chose the best, your father. I married for love. And if you'll not let the good deter you from the best, you'll be a happy woman."

I looked at Mama a little differently than ever before. I reached over and hugged her. And I locked her words in my heart.

I'm sure she meant to give me a confidence toward Martin. But before I could allow that to happen I had to be sure. Was Martin the good or was he the best? I forced myself to imagine life with Arliss. Could it be that he was really the best? Life with him would result in the fulfillment of all my writing dreams. As Martin spent Christmas with us I tried to see him through fresh eyes.

Christmas day brought a gust of cold. We all sat around the fire singing carols, ate a hearty ham dinner and opened presents. Christmas night Mama sat next to Papa and quietly knitted. Papa was smoking a pipe regularly now and sat for long periods of time with it. Once in a while he took his long pipe from his mouth and looked it over as if it was a fine new piece of farm machinery.

Mae sat on the floor playing with her new doll. She turned to Mama and said, "My new dolly is named 'Emily' like Grandma. What will you name your baby, Mama?"

"We don't know yet dear." Mama said. "It all depends on whether it's a boy or a girl."

Papa withdrew his pipe and said, "Little doubt, is there?"

Mama bit her tongue. "Another girl would suit me just fine," she said. "And if so, I favor the name Abigail."

"Hmph," Papa replied, sticking the pipe back in his mouth.

From then on the baby was unofficially referred to as Abigail, Abby, or by Lucy as Gaily.

On the following Saturday, after exacting promises from Mama to have Papa call me from the telephone at the new courthouse if she needed me, Martin drove me to the train depot for the return trip to Sioux City.

We were no sooner on our way in the wagon than Martin said, "Something's wrong, Ann. What is it?"

I had hoped to keep my concern about Arliss from Martin. Now I didn't know quite what to say. But I felt he deserved an explanation.

"Martin, you do love me, don't you?" I asked.

He pulled the buggy to the side of the road. "Say, something is wrong. Of course I love you. How can you doubt it?"

"Oh, I don't doubt it. I'm just a little confused."

"About us?"

"Martin, don't think ill of me if I ask you to kiss me."

"Now? Here on Main Street?" he asked looking up and down the street. "Ann, you know I've got more people watching my every move than the man at the fair with the pea under the walnut shells."

I remembered how once we longed to dance with each other at the ice cream social before I moved to Sioux City and how Martin explained that though he saw nothing wrong with dancing, he had to be concerned that he didn't cause others to stumble by seeing a minister dance. This was the same thing.

"Can't you believe my love by my words?"

I looked down at the two horses looking impatiently around. I understood. Maybe at the station he would kiss me. I longed for the closeness that a kiss brings, remembering with fond irritation the kiss Arliss gave me.

"Can you tell me what's wrong, Ann? Is it something I've done? Or not done?"

"No, of course not. You've been wonderful. I've just been a little confused." I took a deep breath and began, "There's a man in Sioux City, Arliss Cooper, my writing teacher. I'm sure I've mentioned him. He wants me to go out to dinner with him. To see him socially. He seems to be...well, taken with me."

Martin was watching the horses now. "And what are your feelings toward him?"

"I...I don't know," I said unconfidently. "I don't think I care that much for him. But he's a writer. He understands some things I feel---some things I need the man I love to feel."

"Things I don't feel," Martin said.

"Martin, don't ask me more. I don't know what to say."

Martin looked at me softly then drew me close to him and kissed me firmly. When we parted from the embrace, there stood Mrs. McCavity, not six feet away, her mouth open wide. Martin smiled, tipped his hat, and said, "Good day, Mrs. McCavity." And then directing his attention to the two waiting mares he said, "Giddup, girls."

CHAPTER 20
WINTER-SPRING 1900

By New Year's Eve most of the girls had returned to the Academy from their Christmases at home. The novelty of this particular year's end, plus Lottie's wedding, caused a great deal of excitement.

Every student who had returned was present at the six o'clock wedding. Lottie was as nervous as any bride could be. Yet as the music began summoning her down the aisle she looked as promising and hopeful as the century that lay ahead. Andela and I stood at the altar, each of us dreaming of our own futures. Guiltily I pictured my Spring wedding with first Martin and then Arliss.

For Andela, marriage seemed far away. If she was in love with anyone she hadn't told me. Yet at a special wedding of a friend, such as we were now part of, what single young woman doesn't imagine herself as the bride?

In keeping with Lottie and John's wish, the service was short and the couple soon began their lives as Mr. and Mrs. John Hammond.

By nine o'clock the wedding party had left for the small new apartment John had rented. School was to resume on Tuesday, so a honeymoon would have to wait until summer. Members of the church who hadn't attended the wedding began soon after to show up for the watch night service. It would be the best ever, for on this special night no one wanted to sit home alone, except the few who insisted the new century wouldn't really begin for one more year, until January first of 1901.

Reverend Kirby began the evening with a brief robust song service and then asked for testimonies from those who had a special memory of the nineteenth century they wished to share.

Several of the older men gave vivid recollections of their Civil War days. The younger men, some so recently back from the horrors of their war, were more reluctant to recall far too fresh memories.

Some of the widows picked up the thread of remembrance and told of early years of glory, of pioneering Iowa with their deeply missed husbands. As I listened to the stories, I thought once more how a person's life is like a book. I was listening to books tonight, just as if some far away writer had put this all down on paper.

One of the few young persons to stand was Roger Farnsworth. He gave a stuffy recital of what seemed to me an insufferable boyhood surrounded by doting grandmothers and hired nannies brought in to tutor him, lest he attend public school and be mixed with "the wrong sort." Yet he made it all sound so perfect, as if he was describing the life of a nobleman. I glanced over to Olive Randall. Though not a churchgoer she was one of the ones who had to be someplace on such a special night rather than stuck in her room at the Academy. So after attending the wedding, she decided to stay. Now, her eyes lit up over the words of Roger. I turned to Andela after she and I had both glanced at Olive, and said, "It seems Roger will have another young woman at his heels." As testimonies decreased, Reverend Kirby began to call on those whose stories he thought interesting, but whom he knew to be too shy to volunteer. Of course it made some uncomfortable, but it was as rewarding as finding an old discarded book that no one thought to read, and discovering it to be of great interest.

Several were called on in this manner including Ezra Harper who had turned to the Lord through the efforts of evangelist Dwight Moody. Reverend Moody had just died the previous week and several in the church were still in sorrow over his passing.

Reverend Kirby then asked Mrs. Madison to say a few words. Normally the widow had been a talkative woman, but since Joseph's death she withdrew from much social life. In fact I was surprised to see her in attendance at all. It was a brave move to call on her; if she would respond it could be a good sign that her grief was waning. For a few seconds she sat still as a statue, then rose slowly. After a short cough she said, "I have lived sixty years in this century. I have done all that has been called on me to do. Married, borne sons, worked land, tended my sick, buried my family. Now I am passing into a new century. The philosophers among us would say that I should look to it as a robin in Spring. A new beginning, perhaps. And they may be right. That is what I *should* do. Yet I cannot. I have only words for the young here this evening, particularly the young women.

"Be hardy. Make yourself hardy. Yes, enjoy your good times, cherish your good times. Lock their memory deep in your heart, for one day they will be the medicine that will sustain you. I wish I had garnered more such sustenance."

As she sat down, Eben, sitting next to her stood, and with a quake in his voice said, "May I say a word, Reverend Kirby?"

When the minister nodded, Eben began. "I too have seen the sorrows of life, though not as deeply as some. And I say this: though memories can offer solace for the aged, the young must have other potions. We all stand on the brink of a new century. From it, and from you all, I take my strength, I will look ahead, not behind, for my hope whatever the future holds."

Eben sat down and there was silence. His words were timely, but none of us dared to look at Luke Kirby. Eben was thinking of Mrs. Madison and himself when he spoke, yet those of us who were concerned about

Luke hoped Eben's words would strike in his heart.

Yet, like a political speech, Eben's words were the kind hearers take to heart for the moment as a well spoken word, thinking their highest import for the person sitting next to them rather than themselves.

As midnight approached I took to heart the earnest stories I had heard from those who had lived in the early years of the century. What progress mankind had made. When the nineteenth century began our country was so very young. John Adams was President. Iowa existed only for the Indians---the Omaha, Oto, Potawatomi, Winnebagos, and of course the Sioux.

It had taken courage to conquer the land. It took men like my Papa and sturdy women willing to trust their men and follow them, women like Molly Bullard. I was so proud to be a pioneer girl. I didn't stand and speak that New Year's Eve. But in my heart I held the same joys as those who told their stories.

And now there stood a new hundred years to begin. Surely not much more in the way of progress could happen. But if it did, I wanted to be part of it, see it, blaze its trail, just like Mama had.

It would be a once-in-a-lifetime experience to live on the cusp of a century change. Oh, if only there was some landmark I could set down at the stroke of midnight as proof I had been there and had tried hard to grasp the significance of the moment. If only I could have Martin at my side to share this with him. I envied Lottie. Her decision to marry on New Year's Eve was a thoughtful one. And John would have no excuse for ever forgetting their anniversary.

The new year and the decades to come loomed ahead like a great promise. Within weeks we would all be realizing the great opportunities which were ahead for this twentieth century. Already the city streets had several locomobiles speeding along at twenty or twenty-five miles per hour. Perhaps there were even greater advances to be made in transportation, though most doubted much could be done beyond these steam driven cars.

As Spring approached several of the older girls began to slack off in their studies, knowing they would be graduating soon. Yet I found myself even more diligently at my desk. I loved most of my classes except for Public Speaking, which was enjoyable only as long as I sat at my desk writing my speech. When it came my turn to stand in front of the class and give it, I shrunk back.

My activities seemed as a giant snowball gaining momentum with each turn down the hill. My Academy years were drawing to a close. When I had arrived in Sioux City at sixteen I thought of turning and running home to marriage and Martin. Four years seemed so long. But now graduation day lay ahead like a bud on a rosebush ready to burst into blossom. I was now twenty. Life as an adult was before me.

Mama's pregnancy was drawing to a close. Soon there would be a new sibling in the Bullard house. Elsie had just birthed Emily, Grandma's namesake. And far away in the West, Vina had brought forth Morgan James Stoddard.

My writing continued to progress. I sold another story, to the delight of Arliss Cooper. But he remained determined to court me, and, flattering as it was to be sought after by two men, the day comes when a final decision must be made. What is the good, and what is the best, as Mama put it, must eventually be decided.

The day finally came when Arliss asked me to see him in the parlor after my last class for "a very important word" with me.

As we sat on the large davenport, Arliss took my hand, and before I could withdraw it, said, "Ann, the day of reckoning has come. I want you to hear me out before you say anything, and then I want to give you some time to think before you give me an answer.

"I have just received a letter from the Chicago Tribune. They've seen my work on the Journal and are offering me a job on the editor's desk."

"Arliss, how wonderful!" I said.

"Wait, Ann, before you speak, please hear me out. Yes, it's wonderful. Quite a feather in my cap. Of course I'm going to accept the position. Now I can offer you not only my love and my desire to make you my Mrs. Cooper, but a job on one of the most prestigious papers in the country. You'll have a daily by-line, and I'll let you write what you want. I won't burden you with the society page, unless that's what you choose. And besides all this, you can attend classes at the University of Chicago. The newspaper can even pay for it.

"It's the logical, but rarely offered, next step for a writer. You'll hone your skills to a highly professional state while on the staff of such a paper. You'll be a trailblazer for other women who want to write. You'll have your own desk and a beginning salary of one hundred dollars a month---I've already made it a condition of my accepting the job. It's all yours, all ours! We can be so happy together, Ann, I know we can.

"But don't give me your answer now. I want you to think it over. You're used to thinking in terms of being Mrs. Martin Pritchard. I want to give you time to imagine yourself Mrs. Arliss Cooper, writer, author, newspaperwoman extraordinaire!"

"Those are lofty goals, Arliss," I replied. "You think too highly of me. I'm still just Ann Bullard from a little prairie farm. But I am flattered."

"I don't say all this to flatter you. My days of flattering attractive women are over. I want to marry you."

Two second year women studying at the nearby table perked their ears up at the words. I cringed to think of the talk around the table tonight.

"I'm leaving for Chicago in May. I want to be able to buy two train tickets. Please Ann. You can love me, I know you can. And I will always love and take care of you."

I felt my face warm. I couldn't look at Arliss. This was so impossible. Yet the idea of being an important and well paid writer in Chicago was like a dream come true.

Arliss rose. He took my hands and kissed them, then turned to leave.

At dinner I told Andela of Arliss's proposal. She was quick to say, "Ann, you must follow your heart. The only question to ask is, 'do you love him?' "

After dinner I told Olive of the proposal and she said, "You *must* accept. Any woman who is offered as much and turns it down is a fool." Olive was making social strides of her own since that New Year's Eve at the church. She had begun attending Pilgrim regularly, and joined the chorus of women trying to gain Roger's eye. And she had achieved some success since the New Year's Service, as he had called on her several times.

The advice for me that came to mind most, however, was Mama's---"choose the best, over the good." Yet the best depended on who I talked to. I tried to imagine loving Arliss. He had said I could learn to, but could I?

When I saw Lottie in class the next day, she voted with Olive saying, "Ann you've been the one around here to tell us we should go after our dreams. I've even heard you tell that to Eben at church. Now you have a chance for your dreams to come true. Surely you wouldn't choose being a preacher's wife in some small church where you'd be the maid, Sunday school director, and chief volunteer for every project, when instead you could be a famous writer---your dream since childhood. What kind of choice is that?"

I had to admit the sound of each choice gave little doubt as to what I should choose. But still there were Mama's words, "the good is always the enemy of the best. Choose the best."

For the next several days I couldn't write a thing, except my journal entries. During writing class I couldn't look at Arliss. In the evening I would lay on my bed and think. Yet no matter how much I thought, I couldn't make myself know what was right. When I considered marrying Martin, I saw all the things Lottie said, with no time for writing. If I thought of marrying Arliss, I saw all the acclaim, but I felt as though I had a stone in my heart.

The day Arliss proposed I knew instinctively what my answer should be. But as days passed and I entertained more and more thoughts of Chicago, I wavered.

But if Arliss's proposal sent a sharp quake through my life, it was as a mere pebble compared to the days that would soon follow. For one Tuesday morning in mid-April the telephone in the hall rang for me.

Martin was calling from the Courthouse telephone in Stebbinsville. Mama was having premature labor pains and Doc Matthews was concerned. It was still a month early. If the baby came soon, the doc was doubtful it could be saved. Mama wanted me to come.

CHAPTER 21
SPRING 1900

The train ride to Stebbinsville seemed the slowest trip home yet. I pictured Mama lying in bed, perhaps already having given birth by the time I reached home. I prepared myself for what could very easily be a repeat of the tragedy we'd faced two years ago with a miscarriage. This time, though, it would be harder. This baby was nearly full term. To lose it now would be almost like the death of little Benny, Mama's first born.

His death had been so hard for her. I don't think she ever really got over it. And now this baby at almost full term, and most certainly her last, would be a very special child. It just had to live. I despaired for Mama if it didn't.

Of course, such outcomes are in God's hands ultimately. I looked out the window to the waving prairie grass and prayed,

"Dear Lord, please let this child live. And let it be set apart for you." It was a prayer that calmed me. It was as if I knew God had heard and was saying to me personally, "Yes, this child shall live and be for My purposes."

I then thought to pray about Arliss and Martin. Seeing Martin was going to be good for me. The miles separating us made it difficult for me to keep a proper perspective. I liked the busyness of Sioux City. Perhaps I would even like a city the size of Chicago. And the chance to write for pay! It was a grand opportunity indeed.

But as the train pulled into Stebbinsville and I saw Martin standing on the platform, loneliness for me written in his eyes, I was drawn back to the love in my heart for him which had been there the day I left home almost four years earlier. I had grown, changed, matured. But had I grown out of that love, or more deeply into it? That was the question I would have to answer.

"I've missed you more than ever this time," he said. The closer your final return gets, the harder the wait. I just wish this trip were under different circumstances."

"I know," I said. "Is there any news? Has the baby come yet?"

"No. But Doc Matthews is worried. Your mother is bleeding. He can't tell if it's her or the baby. He's with her now. Her labor pains have stopped."

Martin was silent for a few seconds then said, "Ann, you'd better understand the situation before we get to the house."

"What do you mean?"

"Doc Matthews isn't sure both of them can make it. If the bleeding's from your Mama, it could be serious for her."

"She'll be all right," I said sounding as confident as I could. "She's been through this before."

Martin took my hands in his and looked squarely into my eyes. "Ann, we're all hoping for the best, but prepare yourself for anything."

I didn't answer. Mama had to deliver this baby and live. There was no other choice. If God was in control, then surely He knew that the best must happen at the expense of the good. And the best was that this baby live and Mama be there to raise it.

We rushed to the house, where Papa sat stoically smoking his pipe. Grandma was in the kitchen trying to keep Lucy and Mae busy. Papa just nodded at me as I entered, his mind clearly on Mama's welfare for a change.

"Martin, will Doc Matthews let me see Mama?" Then without waiting for an answer I went upstairs and into her room without knocking.

Mama was asleep, Doc by her side.

"How is she?" I asked.

"I've stopped the bleeding, I think," Doc said. "But Ann, she's not very strong."

"And the baby?"

"The baby is still moving, so the signs are good. But your mother needs to start labor again, and soon, or I'm going to have to take the baby through surgery."

"Isn't there anything that can start her labor?"

"I've given her a little something that is supposed to do the trick, but so far, no success. We just have to wait."

And wait we did. All that night and most of the next day we sat and alternately worried and prayed and hoped.

Most of those hours Mama spent asleep. Doc said it was the best thing for her, she'd need her full strength when labor began, so he asked us to simply let her rest. I looked in on her from time to time, usually when she was asleep, lest I tempt her to talk. I too wanted her to just rest. There would be time for talk later.

Early on the second morning after my arrival Doc Matthews came downstairs and said with a deep breath, "Her labor has started again."

We were ready to sigh a breath of relief, but Doc continued, "But I'm afraid the onset of labor has also started the bleeding again. I'm trying to stop it, but I need an assistant. Ann, your mother is asking for you, so it would be ideal if you could help me. And Mrs. Dauber, perhaps you'd better come too."

As we entered the room Mama's face brightened at the sight of me. She held up her hand as a signal for me to take it. I said, "Mama, it's so good to see you awake and smiling. Doc has asked me to help him."

Doc came up behind me and said, "Ann, I really think you can best help by doing what your mother wants.

Your grandmother can assist me. I don't really need your aid, but I wanted to get you up here alone. Your mother wanted to see you---just you, for right now."

"Then there's no bleeding?"

"No, Ann, that was the truth. I'm doing my best to control it, but if there's going to be labor, there's going to be bleeding. I suspect this baby has caused a rupture internally."

I looked at Mama. Her hair was down, draped over her shoulders and her breast. Her eyes seemed tired, her color pale, and beads of sweat had formed along her brow.

Doc Matthews began giving Grandma instructions. I reached for a damp rag on the bedside table and wiped Mama's forehead.

Mama took my hand and said slowly, "Ann, if this is as serious as it seems to be, then I wanted some time to talk to you."

"Mama, you need to deliver Abigail. We can talk later."

Her face suddenly writhed with a stab of pain.

When it subsided she said haltingly, "Ann, listen to me. This baby will soon be here and God willing, will survive. But I may not. And there are some things I want you to know."

I continued wiping her brow, though more out of fondness than necessity. She lurched again in pain.

"What, Mama. What is it you want to tell me?"

She turned her face away for a moment in agony, then back to me as she said, "Do you remember what I told you last Christmas?"

"About Martin and Arliss?"

She nodded. "Remember I told you to marry for love, *marry for love.* It's the only thing that...." Again her face turned away briefly. "...the only thing that can sustain you. Choose wisely."

"I want to Mama, and I will."

She raised her hand to stroke my hair as another pain jolted her. When it passed, she continued running her tired fingers along my hair.

"I know you will. I know. You're a good girl, Ann. So..."

Her voice trailed off as another stab took hold.

"You want so much to write," she said.

I nodded again.

"But, oh, child, don't put your eggs in such a basket, unless there's love there too." Her voice rose in volume, but cracked with pain. "Your Mr. Cooper must be a mighty fine man, to have chosen you to love. But it's not enough...you must love him too, that's the thing. You *must.*"

Grandma was at the doctor's side with rags, cleaning up an increasing flow of blood. Doc was trying to direct the infant into the world.

"Mama, you must be quiet now."

"Yes, yes, just listen to one more thing...I hope, so much, I hope you do become a writer...it means so much.

"But loving a man is the thing. Not the love of writing, as important as that is...you can succeed at writing and die a lonely woman with a shelf full of books bearing your name. But if you marry a man you love, he'll be there to do for you what neither books nor fame can."

Mama squeezed my hand as the pain increased.

"Ann, ask Papa to come in," Mama said.

"Molly, you're about to give birth here," said Doc. "There's no time...."

Mama said, "I want a few minutes with Sam, Doc."

Doc looked flustered. But the severity of Mama's condition caused him to nod to me.

Papa came upstairs, ashen. He stood beside Mama's bed and she took his hand, smiled and said, "Sam."

Papa knelt at her bedside and rested his head on her shoulder. He began to cry softly. I'd never seen tears from those eyes before. Neither he nor Mama spoke as pain again knifed through Mama.

For what seemed like an eternity the baby fought to be born. If there was ever any doubt as to whether this baby was alive and anxious to taste life, it was dispelled as with a final painful effort the tiny infant burst forth. Within seconds it let out the first round of ear piercing cries. It was the best sound I'd ever heard.

Mama lay back, her eyes closed, holding Papa's hand weakly.

Doc busily attended to the necessities while I toweled up the blood. Grandma wrapped the child in a blanket.

Breathless, Mama asked, "Doc, what is it? Is it healthy?" I'd been so involved in the emotion of the event that I'd forgotten to consider whether the baby was a boy or girl.

Doc looked up from his work and said, "Molly, you gave birth early, you know that. This baby is small, though after what you just went through, that must not seem possible. So as to health, I can't promise anything right now, but I can say, he's a mighty good looking little boy."

Papa looked up.

Mama said, "Oh Sam, did you hear that? We got ourselves a son." She closed her eyes again in contentment.

Papa rose to his feet and looked first at Doc, then me, then Mama. A broad smile broke out on his face. "Well I'll be switched," he said. "A boy!"

He walked over to Grandma to look at the new bundle of humanity. "A boy," he repeated, "it just don't seem possible, it just don't."

Doc said, "Now Sam, this boy's been through a real battle to get here. Like I said, I ain't promising anything. He's still got a fight ahead of him."

I remembered the prayer on the train and said, "Oh, he'll make it, he'll make it for sure."

Doc then said, "Well, I certainly hope so. Grandma, better let Ann have a turn there, she might as well get started in learning how to help tend this critter."

Grandma handed the blanket-draped baby to me. I felt as if I was holding a bag of diamonds. I walked over to the bed with the baby and put him down to where Mama could see her new son. Doc, meanwhile, began to tend to her again. "Molly, I want you to stop this bleeding, you hear?"

She didn't hear. She was so taken with the baby. She pulled the blanket back and looked at his face, then turned to Papa and said, "I've had a name for this son on my mind for some time. I want us to call him Jonathan. It means 'the gift of God.' "

"Then Jonathan it is! Jonathan Bullard!" Papa said.

Without looking up from Mama, Doc said, "They'll be wantin' news downstairs. And I'm wantin' Molly to rest now. You all take that baby down, show it off some and then let him have some rest too."

Papa and I walked downstairs together. Papa was beaming like he had borne Jonathan himself.

Everyone looked at us expectantly. Davey sat on the floor, Cory at his side with some blocks. Elsie was nursing Emily. Martin stood on the opposite side of the room, deep concern lining his face. Midway down the stairs with all eyes on us, Papa said, "Well, we done it. This baby here is *Mr.* Jonathan Bullard!"

There was a chorus of great hurrahs all around and then Elsie asked, "And Mama, how's she?"

"Doc's with her now," I said. Then added, "but she's going to be all right, she just has to---she's got a new mouth to feed!"

But as the day wore on and finally turned to evening Doc remained upstairs with Mama, not telling us anything or even making appearances other than every so often for more coffee.

We all slept uneasily that night. Little Jonathan was tucked into his crib in what had been the room I had, overlooking the back of the house, and beyond, the prairie.

Grandma, Elsie and Emily were sleeping there too. Davey and Cory were with Lucy and Mae.

Martin had fallen asleep upright on the sofa. I had been napping restlessly in a chair.

It was past midnight, possibly three in the morning. I awoke and couldn't sleep anymore. I walked to the parlor window and looked down the street towards the shops of town. The soft glow of the new gaslights along Main Street shone above the silhouettes of the buildings.

All was silent. Such times of the night have always seemed to me to carry a special wonderful mysterious feeling, as if the whole world, except God and you, are asleep.

I watched out the window for a long time, thinking, wondering, dreaming. About the present joys and the future---what would it hold for us all?

For the immediate future, plans would have to be made.

Doc had allowed Mama to nurse Jonathan twice but thought we should try to make other arrangements. He didn't like the idea of her nights being bothered by such feedings. There was the uncomfortable idea of bottling milk like some new mothers were doing. The best solution seemed to point toward Elsie who still was nursing her four month-old Emily. That would mean that either Jonathan had to go stay out on the farm with them, or Elsie would have to stay in town for a while. I decided to speak to Elsie about staying for a few days. It was the best solution until Mama regained her strength.

CHAPTER 22
APRIL 1900

Mama didn't regain strength. She grew weaker. Doc tried everything he knew, barely setting foot out of our house.

Mama slept most of the time. But once, on the second day, she asked Grandma to come and sit by the bedside and sing "The Great Physician," her favorite hymn, just as she'd done when Mama was a little girl and just as Mama had done for us girls countless times.

From downstairs we could hear all the distinct tones of Grandma's voice. Those of us who knew the words from Mama's repeated use sang along softly.

The Great Physician is now near,
The Sympathizing Jesus
He speaks the coping heart to cheer,
Oh, hear the voice of Jesus.

Your many sins are all forgiv'n
Oh, hear the voice of Jesus;
Go on your way in peace to heav'n
And wear the crown with Jesus.

All glory to the dying Lamb!
I now believe in Jesus;
I love the blessed Saviour's name
I love the name of Jesus.

And when to that bright world above
We rise to be with Jesus,
We'll sing around the throne of love,
His name, the name of Jesus.

Finally, four days after I had arrived from Sioux
City, two days after Jonathan's birth, Doc slowly de-
scended the stairs. His face showed the signs of the battle, and in his eyes was defeat. He made sure we were
all present before he simply said, "I'm sorry, I did all I
could. Molly is gone."

There was nothing around the room but stunned silence.

This couldn't be, I told myself, we all needed Mama.
Especially now with Jonathan. It just wasn't right.

Papa put on his coat, took up his pipe and left the
house without a word. Little Lucy and Mae started to
cry. I sat down next to Elsie and we both just sat silently by each other, leaving Grandma to take up Lucy and
Mae. She was the one who remained steady. She told
the younger girls in a voice meant for all of us, "It's all
right to cry. Your Mama's going to be missed by us all.
But we must remember she's in a happier place now.
She's with Grandpa, and little Benny. And someday
you'll see her again."

They were meant as words of comfort. But as she
spoke, a torrent of tears began to flow from my eyes. It
hurt so.

Martin sat beside me, his arm around me.

Elsie finally said, "It's this land! This stupid, rough,
ungrateful land!" She started to cry, but then stopped
abruptly.

"No, I won't cry. I won't be weak. Weakness is what
killed Mama."

I, too, stopped crying.

Grandma put her hand on Elsie's shoulder. "You
mustn't dear. You mustn't. Your Mama wasn't weak.
And she cried her share of tears. We all have our bur-
dens, our tears."

Elsie stood up and started up the stairs slowly. "I'll get Davey and Cory and Emily and go home. Back to my farm, my husband and the land." She turned to look at me.

"Maybe you made the right choice after all, Ann."

The next morning I sent a wire to Vina. Of course she couldn't come to the funeral and my heart ached doubly for her pain so far away. I ached that she'd never been able to see Mama again.

On Friday morning the sun shone hot, a harbinger of the summer months to follow. It seemed the whole town made the five mile ride to the small cemetery out by the church. There were more than double the tombstones from the last time I had been here, a testament to the toll the West still exacted on those who would brave it, even in these modern times.

Elsie stood rigid and quiet through the service. Hilda stood with Ethan, her arm in his. I watched her attention drift from Martin's words to the two small markers nearby where she and Ethan had left Katrina and Hans. The strange words resounded in my ears, "I am the Resurrection and the Life..." This was life, this was death. Death was a hinge upon which life must revolve, for now, Martin said. Yet no words could ease the pain for any of us. Papa had been without words since Mama's death. Grandma had been the one to rally us to our duties. It was she, not I after all, who convinced Papa to let Jonathan be nursed by Elsie. Grandma would move in as long as Papa needed her, to look after Lucy and Mae. And of course, when I graduated in a few weeks and returned to Stebbinsville, perhaps some other arrangements could be made.

After Mama was laid in the ground we were all to adjourn to Ethan and Hilda's in town for lunch. But first I wanted some time without my family. I wanted to be as alone as anyone could ever be, for just awhile.

As we boarded the surrey, I said, "Martin, I don't want to go back just yet. Would you take me for a drive?"

"Where would you like to go?" he asked.

"I don't care, anywhere. No, wait, take me out by the buffalo wallow, near the old Simpson farm." It was there I had often retreated as a girl to find a place of solitude. It was there I had been going the day my horse Midnight stumbled and tossed me.

We passed our farm house, now occupied by Fred Phillips and his new bride. Memories of years past flooded my mind. Memories of fires, of parties, of pies baking, of laughter, of tears, of an angry father punishing his girls unjustly, of Mama.

Past the farmhouse lay more of the open land, today a sea of grass waving gently to us, beckoning, cautioning me to treasure it too among my memories.

The town may change, but the land, the rich, rough land stays the same. And to Elsie, exacting a harsh payment for the privilege to live off it, the land seemed the cause of all our grief. But I couldn't blame this land, nor would Mama. We were all put on the land to love it and to tame it. Molly Bullard had been faithful to that.

We came to the place near the buffalo wallow where Midnight had fallen and Tom Simpson found me. I could picture the scene again as if it was only last week. I could imagine seeing Tom again, his voice asking me if I was hurt. For that moment I wished I could go back to that time. Life was much simpler then, even with the problems that had seemed like enormous mountains.

Martin stopped the surrey. I got down and walked toward the wallow. "I'll just be a minute," I said.

The scent of Spring echoed the sweet smell of the flowers we had just set on Mama's grave. The air was quiet and hot. All Earth seemed to be aware of my thoughts. I stood still and tried to think of Mama as a young woman, even before we had moved to Iowa. She was pretty. She was vibrant and alive. I was angry that death would rob Jonathan of knowing his mother. Yet without Mama's suffering that pregnancy, Jonathan, and the gift of God he was, would not have been. If Mama was here, she would have told me how worth it it was to her to die in giving birth to another person.

After a few minutes Martin came up behind me.

"Let's walk a while," he said.

He took me across the road to the shores of Mercy Creek. The water was getting low as it did every year when summer approached. From the distance we could hear the gentle croak of a frog, then a faraway bird called to us.

When we came to a fallen log we sat for a while and listened to the quiet ripple of the water coursing over the rocks.

After a few moments, Martin asked, "When do you have to go back to the Academy?"

"Tomorrow would be best. I've missed more than a week of classes already. Grandma has everything here under control."

"I'll drive you to the station."

I nodded my assent.

"Ann," Martin took my hand, then said, "as difficult as this time is for you, tell me, how do I stand? This fellow in Sioux City, has he taken your heart?"

I thought long and hard about my reply, and remembering all Mama had told me, I said, "Martin, you're the dearest person to me on Earth. Where you go, I will go, where you lodge, I will lodge, your God shall be my God."

Martin bent over and kissed me. It wasn't the kiss of declaration he had displayed in front of Mrs. McCavity but it was one of the most memorable he ever gave me.

Martin took me to the station the next morning and I boarded the train with a heavy heart. Now that the decision was firm in my mind, I wanted to stay with Martin. The next several weeks of school would be even longer than the previous years.

As we waited at the station we decided on June 23 as a wedding date, just two months away. We would be married in our little church, but I wanted Reverend Kirby to perform the ceremony if he could make the trip.

175

Graduation ceremonies were to take place Friday, May 25. Martin would then finally meet Reverend Kirby, a meeting I had wanted for a long time. In all my four years Martin had never been to my Pilgrim Presbyterian. I was anxious to show them off to each other.

This would be the last such trip I would take. As I waved the last good-bye to Martin, I called out, "And keep an eye on Papa. I worry about him."

Martin stood watching the train gain motion, nodded, and waved until out of sight.

I took my seat on the train praying, "Dear Lord, let these next weeks pass quickly."

CHAPTER 23
SPRING 1900

There was an outpouring of sympathy awaiting me in Sioux City, both at the Academy and at Pilgrim Presbyterian. Andela, having lost her father a year before, was especially consolate.

"It is strange, isn't it?" she said. "When our parents die, we advance to the front of the line?"

"What do you mean?" I asked.

"For as long as a parent lives they are like a shield between us and the grave. It is only as a parent dies and we assume their role that we face our own mortality."

Andela was putting words to a feeling that I hadn't been able to express. But, yes, with Mama gone, Elsie and I were the senior women in the Bullard family. Grandma Dauber was still there, but it was like our own lot in life was now advanced to a new position.

And, as my days at the Academy were waning I felt a new maturity ahead. The sands of time were suddenly shifting for many of us.

Roger Farnsworth had met his match in Olive Randall and they were to wed in the fall. Olive would return to the Academy next year as Mrs. Roger Farnsworth, a married student, who took her classes at the Academy and then went home to a husband every evening. Only third and fourth year students were permitted to be married and only five had done so, including Lottie Hammond. Others who had married discontinued their education in favor of their new status as wives.

Lately, even Andela had been enjoying a brief social life. Eben Snow, who had carried her lace cross with him to his duties in the war, had called on her twice.

The time had come for me to end any and all speculation in Arliss's mind. He had plans to make and I would be unfair to delay any longer.

During my first class with him after my arrival back, both he and I seemed nervous. I dropped my pen twice and spilled ink badly the second time. After class he came to my desk and said, "This past week has been a taste of what life without you would be like. I couldn't bear it!"

"Arliss, let's talk. Meet me in the parlor in a few minutes," I said firmly.

"I don't care much for the sound of this. You don't seem as though you've missed me. Though I suppose under the circumstances, you had other things on your mind."

I didn't want to hurt Arliss, yet he left me no alternative. I knew I could never love him as I loved Martin. I would take Mama's last advice to me. She'd never been wrong in her wisdom.

I went to my next class, Deportment, and asked Miss Button to allow me a ten minute tardy.

Arliss was waiting when I entered the Parlor.

"Perhaps this talk is not necessary, Ann," he said.

"You know my answer then?"

"It is in your eyes."

"Arliss, I'm sorry. And I'm honored. You are a wonderful man and a great teacher. If I ever succeed as a writer, it'll be because of these last two years with you. You're a wonderful friend. I'm going to miss you."

"Then your answer is final?"

I nodded.

"My train leaves on the twentieth, will you at least see me off?"

"Do you think that's a good idea?" I asked.

"Probably not, but it gives me one more chance to see you. Please?"

178

"Yes. I will do that. I want to wish you well in Chicago."

"It won't be the same without you."

He bent forward giving me a kiss on the cheek, then turned and left. At the end of the day's classes Miss Button summoned me to her office.

She rose from her desk when I walked in.

"I haven't had a chance to express my deepest sympathy in your recent loss. I'm so sorry about your mother."

"Thank you. It's been a difficult time."

"If you wish I could arrange for you to graduate early. That is, if you're needed in Stebbinsville."

"I thought about that possibility. But I want to finish with my friends. And Mama would want it that way."

"Yes, of course."

After a moment I said "Is that all, Miss Button?"

"Yes, I suppose it is."

As I turned to leave she said, "Well, there is one thing." She sat down at her desk.

"Yes?"

"Ann, sit down a moment."

I did as she asked.

"If I may be so bold as to ask, what was your answer to the young editor?"

"I told him no."

"Any regrets?"

"Oh, not really. But I suppose I will miss the golden opportunity he offered as writer."

"You want very much to be a writer?"

"Yes. It is probably as important to me as the Acadmey is to you."

"That's quite an endorsement. And you think the Academy, even a job in Chicago, are the avenues for you to become a writer?"

"For training, yes."

"Perhaps so. But, as I understand it, the real training of a writer comes not in the classroom, nor even behind the typewriter, but in the thick of life itself. Permit me, if you will, one last lesson for you. And I offer it tuition

179

free," she said smiling.

"You came to the Academy for an education, an honorable pursuit. But what is an education, Ann? Is it really the knowledge that comes from books, or is it the wisdom to live our lives as God meant us to? For many, four years at the Academy proves the forum for them to gain some of that wisdom. For others, perhaps for you, the real education happens to us when life unfolds as a grand and wonderful experience of pain, love, comedy, and tragedy. That is true education. Some of the young women here at the Academy will graduate with honors, and in certain respects we'll consider them educated. But their lives will never measure up to what they could have been, because in all their learning, they've never acquired the very thing I've sensed about your mother as you've spoken about her and as I met her.

"Wisdom, Ann, that's what it's all about. Women like Molly Bullard have an education we simply can't compete with here at the Academy.

"You have made a choice about whom to marry. And you had to consider your loss of writing advantage. A young woman, very much like yourself, had a similar choice thirty years ago. She could have married a fine, strong, young greenhorn who had nothing to his name but his youth and a vision of a ranch he would someday own. But this young woman chose an academic career, with all the security and prestige that it offered. And because of that choice, I have remained *Miss* Button to this day. I've not had an unhappy life, mind you, and I've learned to accept the results of my choice. Still, if I had it to do over again..."

Miss Button stopped. "I just want you to know I think you made the Molly Bullard decision and that you'll never regret it."

"Thank you, Miss Button. Very much."

Andela, of course, approved of my decision. Olive and Lottie were skeptical. The latter was just happy I was getting married at all---she loved her new life, though her grades were certainly suffering.

180

And, as our last week of school approached we all became conscious of grades and our studies. For most of us, this was the last time we would feel the pressure to study and to do well on tests. When it was over, two days before graduation, Lottie invited Andela, Marian Sharp, and myself over to dinner.

She met us at the door as she was about to send John out. She told him tonight's dinner was "girls only" and sent him home, only eight blocks away to visit his parents.

"At least they can be good for something," she said as she closed the door. Lottie, outspoken that she was, had already had more than one encounter with her mother-in-law.

Lottie had prepared an excellent meal which we all compared favorably with Milly's cooking.

As the evening wore on, we talked about our past four years together and our hopes for the future.

"I can't believe it's finally here!" Marian said.

"Neither can I," said Lottie.

"College graduates!" I said.

"Are any of you concerned about what's to happen next?" Andela said.

"Not me!" Lottie said. "In a year I'll probably be a mother---that's my future---and I'm ready for it."

"And you Marian?" Andela asked.

"Wish I knew," she said. "I'll move back home and teach in one of the schools, I guess."

"Ha! Until someone asks you to marry him!" Lottie said.

"What about you, Andela?" Marian asked. "Back to Spillville?"

"Well, I..." Andela looked down at her plate. "I shouldn't say...."

"Oh come on, girl," Lottie pressed. "We're all friends here. What would you do if you could do anything in the world?"

Andela glanced at me and said, "Well, I should not say. But...I would become Mrs. Eben Snow."

Lottie said "Well, I'll be! So even you have a man on the line!"

Andela left herself open for generous teasing with such a confession, but I knew that if she was bold enough to admit it to us, she must really mean it.

Finally to take the teasing off Andela I said "Doesn't anyone want to know what I'll do?"

"Oh we know about you," Lottie said.

"Yes," Marian agreed. "You'll go back to Stebbinsville, marry that preacher, and spend the rest of your life playing second fiddle to all the fussy old ladies in the church."

"No," said Andela quietly, "Ann will marry Martin, yes. But she will write and there will be a novel---a Civil War novel. And we will all be very proud of her, telling our friends someday about this very night, when as young college girls we sat around a supper table and dreamed our dreams."

We were all silent for a while. What Andela said was true, at least the part of some day looking back on this very night.

Finally Marian said wistfully, "I wish we didn't have to grow apart as people do when their common experience, like school, ends."

"Yeah, me too," said Lottie. "I'll miss you all terribly."

"We will all keep in touch," Andela said.

"Oh people say that, but they never do," Lottie said. "Marian's right. Tonight's good intentions will fade away---probably beneath a load of our husband's laundry."

"I've got an idea," I said.

"Yes?" Andela said.

"Let's try to keep in touch, try hard. But if we don't--- if indeed our husbands' laundry obscures our intentions, let's make a pact---a reunion pact."

"What?" Marian asked.

"A reunion. Let's plan to meet again, no matter what, no matter how out of touch we get with each other. As long as we set a date and know it's certain that the other three will be counting on us, we'll keep it."

"But when?" Lottie asked.

"Oh, how about ten years from now? On graduation day, 1910."

"Oh, come on," Marian said. "I can't even remember my own birthday. How'll I ever remember that?"

"Either you vow to remember or we'll carve the day into your hide!" Lottie said.

"Then it's set," I said. "Do we all agree?"

Each one nodded.

"Where will it be?" Andela asked.

"At the Academy, I suppose. Miss Button won't mind," I replied.

"But, what if Miss Button is no longer around, if you know what I mean. She's getting old," Lottie said.

"Well, we'll still meet at the Academy---at ten o'clock in the morning---and if we can't meet there, we'll just go somewhere else," I said.

"Then this is for certain?" Marian asked.

"For certain!" I said. "No excuses."

"Do we bring our husbands? And our children?" Marian asked.

We all thought her question over. Finally Lottie said, "Let's just us meet first, without our families, so we can at least talk together and reminisce, without having to mind children. Maybe we'll then want to get our families together later."

So the pact was made, each of us noting the date firmly.

I think we all parted that night with one more reason to make good.

As Andela crawled into bed an hour later she said, "I am happy for the pact. But let's not lose track of one another during the years."

"No," I said. "We mustn't."

It was the next morning when I sealed my marital decision by standing with Arliss on the platform at Burlington Station.

"Sure I can't get you to change your mind?" he said.

"Very sure. And it won't be long until you'll be glad I decided as I did. Some young Chicago woman will come along and sweep you off your feet."

"I hope she reminds me of you."

"She'll be all you can hope for, I'm sure. Martin is that to me. And this departure is what will cause your path to cross with that one woman. It's strange how God manipulates circumstances in our lives to bring us to just that one person. Martin had a choice of four churches to pastor several years ago. Yet he chose a new congregation just forming out of some small, remote town called Stebbinsville, Iowa. The other three choices were all more attractive, yet as he thought about it and prayed, he felt what might be called a divine nudge toward Stebbinsville."

"I rather wish he'd been nudged to one of the other choices," Arliss said with a smile.

"No, you don't. If that happened you might never get to meet this young lady waiting for you somewhere in Chicago."

The hiss of escaping steam was increasing as the conductor stepped off the train momentarily and said, "You'd better board, sir, she's ready to leave."

Arliss leaned toward me and asked, "May I?" and without waiting for an answer kissed me softly.

I watched as his train and my chance to make a career of writing pulled away, its reluctance seeming to beg me to reconsider. Arliss waved until he was out of sight.

Rather than take the railcar back to the Academy, I decided to walk. The hour would be well spent just being alone.

But several blocks from the station I realized that if I turned left and walked just a few blocks out of my way I would be close to where Catherine Bonacre was now living with her young man.

Would it be right for me to visit?

When Andela and I last visited her, she resented our

184

coming. Clearly she had no concern for me. She was rejecting values I held dear by living with this young man of hers. Such an arrangement was unheard of in Stebbinsville, and women who thought otherwise were asked to leave town.

But I was going to be a minister's wife and maybe even a writer. Either reason would justify my calling on Catherine again.

I approached her building with a butterfly-filled stomach. It was about noon and my walk had made me tired and hungry. Perhaps I should forget Catherine and hurry back to the Academy, I thought---if I walked fast I might yet make the last of lunch.

Just as I considered turning around I noticed a large young man coming out of Catherine's building carrying a crate. He turned and walked almost past me before I impulsively asked, "Are you Buck?"

He looked at me with suspicion and said, "I might be. Who wants to know?"

"I'm Ann Bullard." I said cautiously. "I'm a friend--- well, that is, an acquaintance of Catherine's."

"Oh you are, are you?"

"Yes, I was...walking from Burlington Station and thought of Catherine."

"Well, you can forget about her. Just forget about Catherine Bonacre."

"Have you, uh, had a falling out?"

"A falling out! Ha, that's a rich one, lady. Real rich. The only falling out was done when Catherine walked out on me yesterday afternoon."

The butterflies in my stomach turned to a sick feeling.

"She's left you?"

"You heard me. Gone. She's gone. And I'm moving out, too."

"How....?"

"I was drunk. We fought. She left. It was real simple."

"Where did she go? To her uncle?"

185

"Ha! He wouldn't have her. I don't know where she went, and I don't care. But let me say this---she's got our son and she better bring him up a fighter, a man who can handle hisself."

"A son! When?"

"Two months ago. Say, are you the one what painted the picture?"

"No, that was another friend. Is the picture still there ---in the apartment?"

"Yeah," he said with a smirk, "it's still there. That picture was real nice. Catherine would sit and look at it for hours sometimes. Couldn't figure that woman out. Sit and stare, at a picture like that. It just don't make sense."

"Buck---Mr...I'm sorry I don't know your last name..."

"I don't use my last name, it's just Buck. What do you want?"

"Do you mind if I take the picture?"

His smirk returned. "You do that. Go right ahead and take it."

When I got to the room that had been Catherine and Buck's I understood the smirk. There against the wall of the naked apartment sat the lone picture, a large X slashed through it.

If only I could have helped Catherine. If only I'd known what to do. Now she was out there somewhere with a two-month-old child.

With clouded eyes, I returned to the Academy with the torn portrait in my hand. I gave it to Andela with the explanation. We both went to Miss Button with the news. She said, "Some people will not be happy. They have chosen misery and without even realizing it, they hold their troubles close, nursing them, just as a mother does her baby.

"I'm afraid we cannot do for Catherine what she will not do for herself."

Andela was so touched by Catherine's pain she began piecing the portrait back together. "If it can be saved, I will do so. If I never see Catherine again, I want to

186

remember her. But I want to remember her as I have painted her. For I will always believe it is the true Catherine," she said.

CHAPTER 24
SPRING 1900

Graduation was scheduled for three o'clock the next day. Many of us had relatives arriving on trains throughout the morning. From Stebbinsville I had a contingent which included Martin, Lucy, and Mae. Grandma was staying at Elsie's again and helping with the two babies. There was no possible way they could come, and I understood. I had hoped beyond hope that Papa would respond to my invitation. I received no answer. But I knew my Papa so well that I held little expectation of seeing him.

On one of the earliest trains Mrs. Wersba and Pavel arrived. They had ridden most of the night from eastern Iowa. Many of the first and second year students had gone home for the summer and their rooms were made available to relatives. Others, such as Marian Sharp's family and Lottie's father and stepmother, stayed at local hotels for the night.

At noon I took the railway car to Burlington Station. I couldn't bear to wait until the streetcar brought my people to the Academy. I would meet them at the station and have the ride with them.

The train was late, but when it finally arrived it was worth the wait. First Lucy, then Mae, then Martin stepped onto the platform with hugs aplenty. Then from behind came a familiar limping figure. Papa! He had come to my graduation! Our eyes met and for a second I was reticent. Then I grabbed him and gave him a hug, and said, "Thank you Papa, you came!"

He loosened himself from my embarrassing hug and said, "There has never been a Bullard graduate from a high dollar Academy before. That is reason enough to come!"

His words were true enough. Yet there seemed a new brokenness about him that could only be accounted for by the loss of Mama. He had been so quiet after her death. Now he was beginning to speak again.

The railway car ride to the Academy was dominated by questions from Lucy and Mae who had never seen a city before. Their eyes were saucers taking in every sight, every tall building.

Mae was the first to say, "Ann, can I study at the Academy some day?" I looked at Papa and he said, "Yes sir. I always said to Ann, an education is a mighty fine thing. Why, if it wasn't for me, I doubt she'd ever come this far."

I settled Papa and Martin into a room together and spread out bed clothes for Lucy and Mae on the floor of Room K.

The next morning I introduced everyone to my family, but I gave special importance to making sure all my people knew Andela, Pavel, and Mrs. Wersba. Pavel looked around the Academy with a kind of envy. It represented something he had given up.

At three o'clock the march of the women down the two side aisles of the garden began. We crossed paths in the middle front of the small grassed area and took seats behind chairs where the faculty and Dr. Sinclair sat.

Reverend Kirby gave the invocation and offered some traditional words about our facing of the future. After the ceremonies I would introduce him to my family, and especially to Martin.

Miss Button spoke next, presenting the graduating class of Sioux City Academy for Young Women to Dr. Sinclair. He then rose and called each woman's name in alphabetical order. As we singly came up to receive our diplomas, a handshake from Dr. Sinclair, and a kiss from Miss Button, we felt a swell of pride we'd never known.

My only ache was right after Loretta Anderson's name was called, mine came next---where Catherine Bonacre's should have been. Only a handful of us noticed it--- Miss Button, Andela, and myself.

After Dr. Sinclair's presentation we listened as he gave his brief address to the class---the exact same one we'd heard three times before.

Then Laura Davis, valedictorian, gave an address. How I respected her. She had the highest grades of us all and was so personable.

The last event was a class photograph which was to be mailed to each of us in a couple of weeks.

As the ceremony ended and we adjourned to the parlor for refreshments, a cloud cover advanced over the city. In a few minutes a light rain began to fall.

Inside, the happy hum of voices along with handshakes and hugs and much gaiety went on in spite of the dreary weather outside.

Martin and Reverend Kirby were discussing the wedding to follow in June. Papa was listening patiently as Mrs. Wersba tried to tell him in broken English what a nice Christmas we'd had in Spillville a year earlier.

Lottie led John around by the hand, introducing him to the women who hadn't yet met him. Her father and stepmother were caught up in conversation with Dr. Sinclair.

I watched Andela standing off to the side with Pavel ---they looked lonely---but then from the far side of the room I saw Eben advance toward Andela. I hadn't even noticed he was there. He and Pavel shook hands as Andela introduced them.

It was all so perfect, save the absence of Mama.

Marian Sharp walked up to me and said "Congratulations, Ann---we did it!"

Just then Lucy and Mae tugged at my dress wanting me to escort them to the table for more cake.

190

It was no surprise that an hour later when Papa offered to take us all out to dinner, none of us could think of eating. So the evening was spent visiting at the Academy. At eight o'clock Miss Button handed me a letter and a wire which had arrived earlier that she'd forgotten to deliver.

The letter was from Vina who wished me congratulations and said all was well with her, Charles, and little Morgan. She no longer worked, "unless you consider laundry, cooking, cleaning and childcare work!" she said.

The wire was from James and Julia Evans. James was working for the government in Washington D.C., and had actually spoken to President McKinley. They both wished me well and regretted they couldn't be with us.

I remembered how close we once were---I'd called them my dearest friends in the world and so they had been. I thought of them with each entry I made in my journal. But just as Lottie said the other night---people drift away and make new friends. The book of everone's life contains chapters which you're not in. And though such is how life has to be, to realize it made me sad.

But as long as the chapters continue in your own life, and as long as God writes new characters into your story---who can feel sad for long? Besides, Andela, Lottie, Marian, and I had a pact - we *would* keep in touch.

On Saturday Andela and I took our families on a tour of Sioux City. Mrs. Wersba was delighted. She hadn't enjoyed a city since she'd left Prague more than twenty years earlier. And that night Papa *did* take us all out to dinner and didn't even complain about the prices.

Andela had been bold enough to invite Eben along on our city tour. He and Martin talked easily. I was glad. Eben had no friends, but Martin was always a ready friend to any new acquaintance. Pavel, however, stayed very quiet the whole day.

Sunday, Pilgrim Presbyterian was crowded as several of us brought our families.

Reverend Kirby spoke on the newness of life in Christ, comparing each new adventure we have with the adventures of trusting God.

Eben sat with the Wersba's, coaxing Mrs. Madison to join them. Pavel still seemed ill at ease. I couldn't imagine that he'd be missing his farm work, but perhaps so.

As the service ended, Papa reminded me that we had a train to catch at two-thirty. As we left I hugged each of my church friends. They were characters leaving the book of my life and I would miss them all, especially Lottie and John. They promised they would be at my wedding in a month.

I took a lingering look at the fine church itself. The growth I had experienced in that building, I locked in my memory for future days.

The farewells at the Academy were hardest of all. While Papa and Martin took my belongings down to the waiting horse cab, I said my good-byes to the ones who meant the most to me. Mrs. Whitely had come to the school just to see Andela and me off.

"Do you have any idea how you've influenced my life?" I asked.

"It was all for selfish reasons. If you succeed as a writer I can claim I knew you when you were but a fledgling."

"You can certainly claim more than that! You can claim helping change me from a fledgling into whatever I may someday become."

"Then that will be reward indeed!"

Artemis and Milly were next. I kissed each of them. "Don't ever change," I said to Milly. "You are a wonderful woman. You have a right to be proud." She thanked me and promised to write---a promise she made to all the graduates, but never kept. Miss Button told me she didn't know how to write.

Artemis said, "I don't reckon you can find some kind

words for an old boot like me?"

"You think not? Artemis, I can truthfully say you are a gentleman and I will miss the sound of your third floor voice more than anything I can think of."

"Thank'e, Miz Ann," he replied, then ran to help Papa with the bags.

Finally there was Miss Button.

For a long minute we just looked at each other with a silent understanding. It was like what I'd felt with Mama in the kitchen four years earlier, the day I'd left home. I wanted to say the same thing to Miss Button I had to Mama, "It's not like I'm going away to Africa to be a missionary. I can be back here in only a few hours."

I felt for Miss Button, but I knew that ten minutes after we were out the door she'd be abuzz with preparations for the fall term, going through applications, memorizing names and home towns. She would be ready to start the process all over again.

My good-byes to Andela, Pavel, and Mrs. Wersba were equally moving. Andela would be at my wedding in a few weeks, so the parting was not so hard. I still worried about Pavel. He had not yet returned to his violin. Andela thought perhaps he might never do so.

As I left the steps of the Academy to board the horse cab, I looked back at the beautiful gabled building. On the step stood Miss Button, Milly, Artemis, Andela, Pavel, Eben, and Mrs. Wersba, all waving good-bye. It was of them I now took a mental picture, just as I had done with my family the day I left Stebbinsville. I locked it in place with a prayer, "God, let me never forget this home. Nor these people."

Once the horse cab started, I couldn't look back again. I could only trust the heart picture I had made.

CHAPTER 25
JUNE 1900

Home...How I loved the word. The years at the Academy had sped by just as I had hoped they would. Now I was home again. Ready to take up a part of my life I had left behind.

Time has a way of ripening such experiences so that the richness they possess becomes an even greater joy. I looked forward to June 23 with the eagerness of a child on Christmas Eve, but with the maturity of a woman who now began to make the practical arrangements of being a wife. In only a few weeks I would be cooking every day, doing a man's laundry and loving it. I was going to be Mrs. Martin Pritchard!

I wrote Andela and Lottie and recounted my joy to them. Lottie wrote back in the large words "JUST WAIT" on the back of the envelope as if she knew a secret I didn't. Andela even teased me, so out of character for her. They both were to arrive on June 20. Marian was to arrive on the 21st and many of the Sioux City party were coming on Friday, the 22nd.

Miss Button would arrive on the 22nd and leave right after the wedding, according to her letter. She said no news had been received concerning Catherine. She had contacted the uncle but he hadn't seen her since she took up with Buck. The sad end of her tale would apparently not be known to any of us for some time.

Reverend Kirby thought he would have to perform the ceremony and turn right around and go back, so he could be in his pulpit Sunday morning. But he wrote with news that Luke had volunteered to take his father's place that Sunday.

Needless to say, Reverend Kirby agreed. To see Luke express such an interest was a great fulfillment to his father's heart.

Barely a week before the wedding I received a package from Chicago. Inside was a copy of the Chicago Tribune with Arliss' byline circled in red. Also enclosed was a small burgundy vase with card:

> *Best wishes to the bride and groom*
> *Arliss*
> *P.S. on the train to Chicago I encountered a Miss Beatice Exum whom I have been seeing.*
> *Perhaps she is the woman of whom you speculated. The result of a divine nudge - yes, I can hear you say the words.*

The vase was put into service immediately and the newspaper saved as a remembrance.

As the day drew closer I became more frantic. There was so much to do. All my lessons in Miss Button's Deportment class evaporated. Aside from the wedding duties, there was family to consider. Not just mine; Martin's mother had arrived in early June and would stay until just after the wedding.

Grace Pritchard was older than my Mama, closer to Grandma Dauber's age and like Grandma Dauber, still quite active.

I meant to spend as much time with her as possible, even though each visit meant a lengthy ride out to the parsonage where she stayed with Martin. I wanted to know this woman who had done such a job of raising Martin.

Martin had told me that from his birth his mother had prayed for him to preach and to marry the woman of God's choice.

And to be around Mother Pritchard was to sense the

spirit of a woman who accomplished more on her knees than most women on their feet.

I hoped in some measure to be like her.

Grandma was living in our house with Papa, Lucy, Mae, and me.

Elsie was still nursing and caring for Jonathan, plus her Davey, Cory, and Emily. I didn't see her unless I specifically drove out to the farm. I did go quite often, taking Lucy and Mae to see their new brother.

Jonathan was an active baby. Elsie appeared always on the edge of exhaustion. She was working harder than when she lived at home with us. Often on my trips I would stay with the children and send her into town. She never stayed gone long, and by the time she returned, I had two hungry and fussy babies, waiting for lunch.

Elsie hinted that after Martin and I were married we might want to have a hand in taking Jonathan for awhile. It was decided that as soon as he was weaned, Jonathan would stay with us.

Of course Papa had quite a say in all this---after all, Jonathan Bullard was his pride and joy. But he was ill-fitted to care for a baby, even with Grandma's help. She had all she could do to mind Lucy and Mae.

Martin offered to keep all three children with us if necessary, but Grandma seemed to enjoy her duties at Papa's. She felt needed.

Martin was the calmest of us all during this hectic time. He continued his business as normal, humored by the fuss being made.

Papa continued to tease me as always, but there was a new flavor to all he did. He never demanded of Lucy and Mae what had been required of Elsie, Vina, and me. He was content to let them be little girls while they could. He would do all the manual labor, or it wouldn't be done. As hard as it was to believe, he had finally begun to soften toward what remained of his family.

The hardware was one of the most successful businesses in Stebbinsville; Papa eventually sold Uncle Phil half-interest.

196

Don Matthews had married Florence in the winter and was active in the Merchants Association; he planned to run for mayor. His return to town as a war hero had made a fine man of him. I couldn't help but think Vina was missing out by being Mrs. Charles Stoddard.

The evening of their arrival Andela, Pavel, and Eben sat with me in the parlor where they wanted to speak to me privately.

Andela began, "Ann, it has happened that I am soon to follow your example."

Eben touched Andela's hand with his own and continued, "I've asked Andela to marry me."

"Well!" I said, "This is a surprise."

"We wanted you to be the first to know." Andela said. "We will be married in August. You will come? You will stand with me, as I do for you?"

"Of course. Nothing could prevent it," I said.

Even Pavel looked happy as he heard the news again.

"So tell me more," I said. "What of your plans after the wedding?"

Eben spoke slowly as was his custom. "I have asked Mrs. Wersba to allow me to buy the farm from her, and of course she will continue to live with us. I will have my farm, and the woman I love."

"And what of Henrietta Madison?" I asked.

Eben looked away briefly. "She has decided to live on alone in Sioux City. I asked her to come to Spillville with us, but she won't. Yet I don't feel I can be a man and not marry the woman I love and not farm as I want to. It has been a hard decision. I will always regard Henrietta as my second mother."

"We will keep in touch, perhaps we will persuade her yet," Andela said. Still touching Eben's hand, and reaching her other hand to her brother, she said, "Pavel, tell Ann your news."

Pavel smiled as if about to reveal a great secret.

"When Eben and Andela marry and assume the leadership of the farm, I will be going to Chicago. To the conservatory."

"I knew it!" I said. "I didn't know how, but I just knew some way you would be able to go...and that you would again play your violin. God wouldn't allow you to waste your talent."

"My thanks to you, Ann. I hope you are right---that the talent is indeed there. Someday I will write a symphony for you."

Immediately I had an idea.

"Pavel, did you bring your violin?" I asked.

"Yes, I believe I owe you some Christmas carols."

"Could I exchange that request? Instead of the carols, would you play for my wedding? I would like nothing more than to come down the aisle to the music of a master musikant."

"I would be honored," Pavel said.

And so another arrangement was made, and another announcement that caused me to be thankful.

That night before the wedding I sat alone in my room looking out the window. The dark hung over the prairie like a warm blanket. In front of me was the journal I had been given four years earlier. It had long been full, but even though I had compiled my thoughts and activities in newer journals since, that first book always remained special and sentimental. I carried it with me in all my travels, as a constant reminder of my yearning to be a successful writer. But now I was on the threshold of a new change. The days of my youth were over. Soon I would be a married woman, with all the changes that implied. What would become of my writing now? Had the desire of my heart been fulfilled? Or would I always be disappointed? As I thought about it, I realized that God *had* given me my heart's desire. My love for Martin was a deeper love than my love for writing. To live my life with him would be a life of fulfillment---the life I really desired. If I never wrote again, I would be just as happy. To serve in this small church was better than writing for all the newspapers in Chicago *or* New York! To have a husband like Martin was the best. Mama had been right, and I knew she'd be pleased.

As I listened to the chirp of a nearby cricket somewhere beneath my open window, I wondered if I should simply close the journal for good and pack it away to be read again some distant day. Perhaps I would continue to record the events of my life, even those of my early childhood which preceeded these college writings. But now I would be doing it for me, for my own children, for my own descendents---to record events of a time which soon would be passed, rather than because of any hope for publication.

New duties would soon be falling to me and I anticipated them with great contentment. I was glad to be back in Stebbinsville, and not in Chicago. Glad to know that in less than twenty-four hours I would be a married woman starting a brand new life. I had chosen the best. I wished somehow God would allow Mama a peek at my happiness tonight.

Perhaps laying the journal aside would mean laying writing aside. I couldn't know the future. I couldn't know how God intended to use my desire to write. Maybe there needn't be more than one Louisa May Alcott. Perhaps he would use my writing in ways I couldn't see. But for right now, I knew I had to chose a life as a pastor's wife, not as a famous woman author. Again it was a choice of the best---God's will for me---over the good.

I wanted my words to be read by others, perhaps others now distant in time and location from me. But that day would have to wait. God would have to determine the use for my writing. For me, my future was at Martin's side.

I held the book close to my heart and remembered the days and nights, the feelings and hurts it harbored. And then I tucked it gently away in my cedar chest beneath my diploma from the Sioux City Academy for Young Women.

The next morning, the one so long awaited, finally came. The preparations had ended. The guests arrived from near and far. I was in the parsonage being helped into my gown by Aunt Hilda. She was older now, the twinkle in her eye had changed. She would never get over the loss of her only two children, but she and Ethan were still so very capable of the love and self-giving qualities they'd always possessed in abundance. I wished Aunt Hilda could have spoken with Henrietta Madison.

When I was nearly ready and the guests were being ushered to their seats by Jed and Don, Papa came in.

"Hilda, may I have a word with my daughter?"

"Yah, sure, but not too long. Is almost time to begin," she said and left quickly.

Papa looked me up and down and said, "Four years can sure make a difference."

I didn't have words.

Papa seemed as nervous.

"Ann, I'm not much with good words, not like you are. But there's times a man's got to try to find the right ones."

He walked over to the window, his back to me.

"What I mean is...well, I'm proud of you. That's what I mean to say. You look real pretty and I'm happy you're my girl. Now, I know you wish your Mama was here to-day---and a poor excuse for a Pa like me can't quite even out the score. But I done some things in my life I'm proud of---I moved you all here when not a one of you was willing. I built a farm, a fine one too. And some years ago I picked me a woman to marry, Molly Dauber. So you see, I done some things I'm glad of.

"And then, well, I know I done some things here and there, that I'm not so proud of. And I got no reason for them, it's just the way I was. I just don't know if I could have done much different---but what I done, I done."

"Papa, I know...."

"Now wait, hear me out. Anyway, I tried to figure out a present for you and Martin---something that I was sure your Mama would have thought real nice, some-thing I figure she would have picked if she was here."

There was a knock on the door and Hilda said, "Dis is

not time for talk. Da wedding, it is ready to begin."

Papa was facing me again now.

"Well, I want you to know I'm going to try to be, well, better to Lucy and Mae. And, as for your present, well I reckon you'll see it soon enough." With that Papa reached over and gave me an awkward kiss.

I found myself wondering if brides are supposed to cry before the ceremony? I leaned over to Papa and hugged him and for the first time in my life he hugged me back.

Then we allowed Hilda back in to fuss over us and get us across the parsonage yard to the church.

I caught the scent of the early summer prairie---no flowers in my bouquet could equal it.

Because it was early summer, the severe heat hadn't yet arrived. It was quite warm, however, and a gentle breeze tugged at my veil as I entered the small quiet church where Martin had first come to preach years ago when I was yet a child.

A woman's wedding day is one of varied emotions. For me, walking down the aisle on Papa's arm, feeling his strength beside me, for the first time a real comfort, and knowing that in the midst of this unspeakable joy there remained a touch of sadness for the one who wasn't there. It was another of those moments one holds in the memory like a fragile rose. Such memories fade so quickly, they must be called up again and again and relived lest they fade away.

As we took that slow walk down the aisle to the beautiful strains of Pavel's violin, the heads of all those I loved turned to watch me. Each was a landmark of my life---from Uncle Phil who had been with us in Illinois from the day I was born, to the Ethan Stones who had been our refuge when we arrived in Iowa, to Miss Button, who sat there smiling, her hankie continually tugging at the edges of her eyes.

And then on my left I saw my present from Papa. The

201

most welcome guests of all---Charles and Vina sat with young Morgan Stoddard starting to fuss for attention. His cries were the sweetest sound of the day. I could hardly contain myself!

I turned almost unconsciously to Papa and whispered, "Thank you, Papa, thank you so very much."

Papa only smiled.

Behind me, walking in the same perfect rhythm to the strains of the Wedding March were Andela, Lottie, and Marian. Ahead of me, waiting, just as he had for four long years was Martin. My Martin.

I watched him as he glanced over the front row to where his mother sat. His eyes were saying, "See Mother, what a wonderful wife the Lord prepared for me. All because you have kept praying."

Across the aisle on my left sat Grandma with little Jonathan in her lap and Lucy and Mae by her side, Mae fidgeting under the lace of her best dress. And Elsie sitting on the other side of Mae telling her to settle down, young women aren't to fidget.

To me I knew she was wanting to say, "At last!" This education business is done and you can get on with your real life." My years at the Academy were, to her, my version of little Mae's restlessness.

Yet it had been worth it to wait. Somehow it made this day that much more special to know a price had been paid.

We stood, Martin and I, in front of Reverend Kirby as he spoke the appropriate words, the same ones I'd heard before, but this time I listened more closely---they were being spoken to me.

"Love, honour, obey....in sickness and in health...till death do you part...."

I felt a breeze through an open window and felt as though Mama was there with me after all, echoing Reverend Kirby's words and adding her own of "choose the best, not the good."

Mama *was* there---in me---in the woman I had become. I was fashioned by Molly Bullard, and her in-

fluence would be with me always. And someday, some
distant day, I would see her again.